BIANCA

ALSO BY JOAN PHIPSON

BIANCA

Joan Phipson

Margaret K. McElderry Books
NEW YORK

Margaret K. McElderry Books
Macmillan Publishing Company
866 Third Avenue
New York, NY 10022

First published in Australia by Viking-Kestrel
First United States Edition 1988
Printed in the United States of America
10 9 8 7 6 5 4 3 2 1

Composition by Haddon Craftsmen
Allentown, Pennsylvania
Printed and bound by R. R. Donnelley & Sons
Harrisonburg, Virginia
Designed by Barbara A. Fitzsimmons

Library of Congress Cataloging-in-Publication Data
Phipson, Joan.
Bianca.
Summary: Finding Bianca wandering the countryside in
a state of amnesia after a devastating emotional scene
with her mother, Hubert and his sister, Emily, wonder if
she would benefit from exposure to their own bustling
family.
[1. Mothers and daughters—Fiction. 2. Amnesia—
Fiction. 3. Emotional problems—Fiction. 4. Family
life—Fiction] I. Title.
PZ7.P55204Bg   1988   [Fic]   88–13192
ISBN 0–689–50448–9

To Margaret McElderry,
guide, philosopher, and friend.

BIANCA

1

It was as the car came over the crest of the last hill and Hubert saw the whole shining spread of water laid out below him that he made his remark. Hubert was given to sudden, unexpected observations. This one took hold of his mind to such an extent that, in consequence, Paul nearly drowned.

"Queer," he said thoughtfully, as he guided the car down the final slope of the rough track that led to the dam, "when you think that water was really the mother of us all. If it weren't for water, you know, Emily, none of us would have existed." He took his eyes off the road in order to look at her more closely. "Not even you, Emily."

If he had hoped in this way to impress her, he was disappointed. "Hubert, for goodness sake keep your eyes on the road. You'll have us in the ditch."

But he was still thinking about it, after they'd left the car, when Paul fell into the headwaters of the dam. He made only a small splash, so perhaps Hubert, absorbed as he was, failed to notice immediately.

It was Emily shouting, "Hubert, quick! He can't swim," and giving him a push, that sent him to the rescue. For a moment his long, seventeen-year-old figure teetered on the bank, and then he went in with a much louder splash than Paul had made. His head popped up again like a cork. He spat some water out of his mouth and said, "Quick, Emily. Where is he?"

"Right behind you," screamed Emily.

By this time Paul was beyond speech. When they got him to the bank he could only cough and gasp as he stared at them with wild and frightened eyes.

"Artificial respiration," shouted Emily. "How do you do it, Hubert?"

But Hubert had picked Paul up by the ankles and was holding him upside down. "Thump him on the back, Emily," he said.

Emily never did things by halves. The results were now prompt and gratifying. When it was over Paul took two enormous breaths and burst into tears. Hubert put him down. "That's that," he said. "Don't do it again, Paul." He turned to Emily. "Good thing he's only five. If he does it again when he's older you'll have to give him the kiss of life—disgusting phrase. I can't say I really know how to do it. Watched it often enough, of course."

Emily was bending over Paul and wasn't listening. "Stop crying, Paul. You're safe now." She had pulled a tissue from her jeans pocket and was about to deal with his face. But when she looked at his dripping hair and sodden pullover she put it back with a sigh. Instead, she picked him up and put him on his feet. "Why did you have to go and fall in?"

"A silly question," said Hubert.

Neither Paul nor Emily took any notice. Even at five, Paul had got used to Hubert. "I was looking for the ducklings." His tone suggested that Fate had dealt with him unjustly.

"There weren't any where you fell in. Hubert had just looked."

"I didn't know. He never said." Paul seemed undecided whether to burst into tears again.

"Even if there had been," said Hubert, "they'd be gone now, with you splashing about among them."

"I never—" This time a howl of despair interrupted his speech.

"Shut up, Paul," said Emily. "Come on. We'll look for some more."

"Oh, don't let's," said Hubert. "Let's go home. I'm all wet."

"Paul's all wet, too, but he doesn't want to go home, do you, Paul? You want to see the ducklings, don't you? After all, it's why we came. And there's our picnic. You want that, don't you, Paul?"

"We could go to the trailer," said Hubert. "Dad usually keeps a few old clothes there."

"'Oh, Hubert, it's miles. That's why we told Dad we couldn't go to check it today. I don't see why he can't look after his beastly fishing trailer himself, anyway."

"Emily, you know—" But Hubert was interrupted.

"Want to see the ducklings," said Paul, and this time the cruelty of life quite overcame him and he burst into tears again.

Hubert groaned dramatically. "Come on, then. The sooner we find some ducklings the better."

They set out along the shore of the dam, single file, to the accompaniment of diminishing sobs.

A short time after the sobs had ceased Emily said, "Paul—" He stopped and turned. "I thought so. Where are your glasses?"

He felt about on his face. "They're gone," he said.

"I can see that. They must be in the dam. Oh, blast. Hubert!"

He had gone on ahead, but her voice stopped him in midstride. "Well?"

"We'll have to go back. Paul's glasses fell off in the dam."

Hubert walked back to her slowly. "You want me to *dive* for them?"

"It can't be very deep."

"It's not only deep, it's muddy. There's not a chance of finding them."

"Doesn't matter. We'll have to go back and look. They might have fallen off on the bank."

"Emily, don't be ridiculous."

"Well, we'll have to tell Mum we looked. Glasses cost money. Come on."

It was easy enough to find the spot again, for the mud from their efforts to get Paul out of the water had not yet settled. "See?" said Hubert. "Apart from being revolted at the thought of diving into that, I'd never see a thing. Be reasonable, Emily."

They walked up and down on the grass, impelled, without hope, by a sense of duty. The glasses were not there. "Can you manage without them, Paul?" Emily asked in the solicitous tones her mother might have used.

" 'Course I can. It's only a long way away everything looks woolly. I can see you, Emily."

Hubert gave a snort of laughter. "And that, you must admit, Emily, is the important thing. Shall we go on, now?"

"We might as well. I can't see any point in looking any more. You are a creep, Hubert."

It was a bright spring day. The slight breeze that brushed their cheeks was crisp still, but there was just a hint of warmth to come—that first, electric promise that life everywhere was stirring again. The grass along the banks was still more brown than green, and bruised with frost, but the promise was there, and if one had knelt and peered at the roots it would have been possible to see here and there little spears of green. The wide sweep of water spread out almost all round them as the dam pushed its way in among the hills. Where they had come, driven by Hubert in their mother's little car, the ground was flat, meeting the water here and there with clumps of rushes. It was here last year that Emily had seen several families of yellow baby wood ducks. And in an expansive and soon regretted moment Hubert had offered to bring Paul on the first fine weekend of spring. They had come with a picnic and high hopes and because the day was so nice, Hubert had almost begun to look forward to a pleasant and relaxing time by the water, mildly enlivened by the small evidences of burgeoning spring. Emily did not remind him that Paul was always an unknown element.

At this time of year there was no one else on, or near, the dam. The water was still too cold for the usual summer water sports, and most people found the shores damp and uninviting. The few farms that clung to the less wooded and flatter parts of the shore had the dam to themselves and were able to forget, until the summer came, the recurring fear of fire that holiday-makers always brought with them. Now the sun shone benignly on the sparkling water and on the dark hills that seemed to guard its innocent surface. There was no sound at all except for an occasional small, wet slap as a ripple arrived at the bank. After the sobs had subsided they walked in silence, and the sun slowly warmed the two wet bodies and began to dry the wet clothes. After a while Hubert and Paul dragged off their pullovers and slowly the morning's peace fell on them again. The damp and fecund smells that rose from the water's edge were somehow stimulating—even a little exciting. Hubert stopped suddenly and bent down.

"Here," he said, and poked his finger into the squashy water weed. "Here, really, is where we all began. This is where our first mother discarded her children and said, 'Go out into the world and make your fortune.' Not all of us did. Curious to think of it, isn't it?"

Emily, who had nearly sent him into the water for a second time by bumping into him, said crossly, "I never know what you're talking about, Hubert. If I didn't know you were supposed to be the great family brain, I'd think you were just plain bananas."

"Bananas," sang Paul. "Bananas, bananas. Hubert's bananas." He had recovered.

"Maybe," said Hubert mildly. "But it's true all the same. Except that it was salt water, I suppose. It always astonishes me. No wonder everyone has such a thing about water. We drink it, swim in it, sail on it—and we're eighty-three percent water, anyway. No wonder we're obsessed with the stuff. It's our homeland—our birthplace—where we belong."

"Well, I don't," said Emily. "When are we going to have lunch?"

"Not till we've found the ducklings," said Hubert, unruffled. They were approaching a small clump of trees that grew by the water's edge. "Last spring I saw two or three mother ducks swimming about with their ducklings just about here."

"You'd think they'd move away from the trees," said Emily. "Crows and hawks and things could sit up there and watch them. A nice breakfast I expect they'd make for a hungry crow."

"So they do. But they can't help starting off near the trees. That's where the wood ducks' nests are—up in the trees—and they come tumbling down when they're ready and take refuge in the tree roots."

"I wonder they don't die of fright." She was marching on with a firm and determined stride, impelled more by the thought of lunch than by the ducklings. But Hubert stopped again suddenly, this time holding his hand up.

"We'll just have a look. Don't want to frighten them."

Paul pushed between them. "Are they there?" His voice was hoarse with excitement.

Hubert shook his head, and for a moment they all stood silent, searching the shadowed water under the trees. It was mirrorlike and still, unruffled even by the mild breeze. Nothing disturbed its surface. They moved forward slowly. They had just reached the first tree, the nearest to the water's edge, when there was a sudden splash, a great fluttering, and a full-grown duck plunged away from the bank, out into the deeper water. It did not seem to be making much of a job of escaping, for it thrashed aimlessly about, flapping its wings and paddling in circles—making a great commotion in the still water.

"Poor thing," said Emily. "I think it's hurt its wing."

As they watched, it managed to move farther from them and after a time its flutterings became fewer and it moved more easily through the water. It seemed to be recovering, but now it was some distance away. Hubert moved forward very carefully and the others followed. Muscular roots clutched the bank, spreading out, holding the tree firm as it towered above them, and where the roots met the water, little red threads were visible below the surface. Among the roots were hollows where the earth had washed away and from one of these, just by the water, there was a sudden scattering, a series of small splashes, and the surface was broken by six yellow blobs that fanned out in all directions, paddling for dear life, cheeping as they paddled. Six small bow waves spread out behind them.

"There," said Hubert. Paul drew in an ecstatic breath and Emily said, "Ah," in a sentimental voice.

Then they watched in silence as the ducklings paddled away. They saw them gradually converging on the point where they had last seen the grown duck. When the last duckling had disappeared round the bank and the waters of the dam had settled to their mirror-calm again, Emily said, "Poor mother duck, having to mind all of them with her broken wing."

Hubert shook his head. "Not broken," he said. "She just wanted us to think it was, so that we'd follow her and leave her ducklings alone."

"Why would she do that? We *like* baby ducklings." Paul was indignant.

"Because she's a mother," said Hubert. "That's what mothers are for."

They found no more ducklings, and the last they saw of those was the small convoy, headed by the mother duck, paddling in close formation away out along the farther shore of the dam.

"They'll come home when we've gone," said Hubert. "Let's have lunch."

The sun was overhead and the dew had gone from the grass. They found a patch of green near an outcrop of rock. Emily spread the pullovers on the rock to finish drying and they settled down with their backs to the rock and with great enthusiasm began their lunch. Very soon a pleasing sense of peace settled on them all. The small breeze had dropped and the waters of the dam were very still. Insects of various kinds, thawed and enlivened by the sun's warmth, hummed and buzzed about them. The surrounding hills lay silent under the sun and on the distant farms the cattle were lying down and all life seemed suspended. The farmers and their families were inside their homesteads, having their midday meal, too.

Time passed, and two at least of the picnickers—Emily and Hubert—were unaware of its passing. It was Paul who eventually and inevitably disturbed the peace.

"Something funny's happening." Paul's voice was far away and made no impression on the two motionless bodies on the grass.

"I said something funny's happening." This time Paul's voice was nearer, higher still, and louder. Emily sat bolt upright. Because he was standing on the rocks directly behind her she did not see him immediately. Nor had the words yet penetrated. It was the ring of urgency that had dragged her from sleep. She looked quickly at Hubert. Then she saw that Paul was gone. She jumped up and looked at once toward the dam. There was nothing to be seen and she had just begun to run when Paul said, "I'm here. Not down there. I said something funny's happening."

"Did you have to wake me just to tell me that?" The sight of him up on the rock, though reassuring, was infuriating.

"Well, look." His finger pointed toward the dam.

She turned again. "I can't see—" And then she realized why she could not see. There was nothing to be seen. Beyond the grass in front of her, stretching down to the water, and a few feet of shoreline, there was nothing to be seen at all. It was as if the whole of the dam, that great sheet of water that should have lain before her, and all the pleated hills beyond were gone. As if the world to the south of where they were had ceased to be. Above, the sun still shone and to the north the sky was blue. But everything south of the zenith had disappeared. Beyond the bank the breeze had dropped by the time they had their picnic, but now it was as if the air itself was petrified.

They knew it was only a mist, caused by the arrival of cool air on the warmer surface of the dam. But it did seem necessary to remind themselves of this. There were no ripples now. The water at the edge of the dam lay quiet in the shallows. Through it the wet mud gleamed. For a small distance sun and mist competed over the still surface. Then water, sunlight, everything disappeared into nothingness. Even the mist was no longer palpable. There was nothing there at all.

Emily and Paul now stood beside Hubert on the bank. They all looked silently at nothing. Then Paul said, "See? It's funny, isn't it?"

"Can't see why it should be so funny," said Emily.

"I can see what he means," said Hubert. "And it isn't only because he hasn't got his specs." He paused, and then said very firmly, "But it is only mist, Paul."

"So what do we do? Go home? I'll pack up the lunch things anyway." And Emily, who saw nothing funny about an ordinary mist, went and bustled about among the empty plastic boxes and mugs.

They did not go home straight away. For a long time

they wandered about doing nothing in particular, glad of the lingering sunshine and looking over and over again at what they could not see of the dam. The trees where they had seen the ducks stood motionless and black beside the water, as if they were concealing secrets. Perhaps they were. Perhaps there were more clutches of ducklings among the twisted roots. There was no sign now of any little flotillas on the water.

Presently, as the sun slipped toward the west and their three shadows elongated across the grass, Emily, laden with baskets, said, "What say we go home now? I've had enough of looking at nothing." Hubert turned his back on the dam and looked at her. He took a step toward her, but then stopped.

"Wait a little longer," said Hubert. "I rather like it." Emily gave an exasperated sigh and sat down on the grass, surrounded by baggage. Paul sat down beside her.

It was then, as Hubert stood as he had stood before with his back to the sun, and Emily and Paul sat behind him, not quite sure if they were watching him or the sightless mist, that there came a movement in the void that confronted them. At first it seemed no more than a thickening—a kind of shadow—in the blankness. Then, more solidly dark, the shadow moved slowly. Hubert and Paul heard Emily draw in her breath. The shadow came toward them. Paul said, "Something's splashing." And the shadow took shape and formed itself into a rowboat. At first that was all that was visible, and it seemed to move of its own accord. But it came closer still, and at last they could pick out a figure sitting on the thwart. It moved rhythmically backward and forward as it rowed, and a small splash came each time the oars met the water. It was quite a small figure and it had long, fair hair that swayed as it moved. They had just one moment to see that it was a girl before she looked over her shoulder, saw them on the bank in the last of the sunshine, swung the boat round, and disappeared again into the mist.

They waited, hoping she might come back, hoping secretly that she would come back and reveal herself as flesh and blood. It had been so quiet—so insubstantial—that brief vision, that their minds were filled with very curious questions indeed. But she did not come back. Instead, the mist, which had remained so totally negative, so formless, now began to give off exhalations of cold air. They could feel it on their cheeks and foreheads. And, very slowly, it crept toward the shore. It began to thicken and become the kind of mist they knew—a moving presence on the surface of the land as well as the water. Involuntarily they all stepped back, and felt the first tiny drops of moisture on their faces. If there had once been a girl in a boat so near them, she was gone now—as if she had never been. No sound came from the thickening mist and the only movement was from the mist itself as it flowed out of the dam and began to blanket the shore.

"What was it?" said Paul.

"Didn't you see it?" said Emily.

"See, I haven't got my specs. Everything looks woolly."

"That's what it looked like," said Hubert. "Woolly."

"But I did hear something," said Paul. "Little splashings."

"Come on. We'd better go," said Emily, "or we'll never find our way home. Who'd have thought this'd happen on a nice spring day?"

"It isn't a nice spring day anymore," said Paul. "It isn't a winter day, either. It's a nothing kind of day."

"Get in," said Hubert, opening the door of the car. "As Paul says, Emily, it's a nothing day, and perhaps nothing really happened. I don't believe that was a girl in a boat. I don't believe we saw anything at all."

Emily was halfway along the track, trudging up with most of the baskets. Rather breathlessly she said, "I don't know what you and Paul thought you didn't see. I saw a girl rowing a boat, and I'd like to know what she thought she was doing, and I'd like to know where she came from and where she went. She certainly didn't want to see us."

Hubert put the baskets in the car. "We'll never know. But we saw the ducklings. That's what matters, isn't it?"

"I didn't want to see a silly old girl in a boat anyway," said Paul. "But we might have seen another lot of duck-lings."

"I expect they were all sitting cozily under their mothers' wings among the roots of the trees," said Hubert.

They entertained themselves with this pleasing thought until they reached the beginnings of the auto track. By the time Hubert had negotiated the rough route out of the hills and had once more found the paved road, they had almost forgotten the last curious happenings of their day by the dam.

2

On that same spring morning their father was sitting, as
usual, in his office in the town where they lived, waiting for
his next patient. He knew that the waiting room was full,
yet there was a longer delay than was normal. He checked
over the material provided by his secretary. The next
should be an old man he knew well. Jack Johnson had been
coming to him almost as long as he could remember. All
he really needed was a checkup, a chat, and a new bottle
of pills. He was always punctual. But it was not Jack Johnson who eventually came through the door; it was his
secretary, and, uncharacteristically, Miss Blakemore was
upset. It took a lot to upset Miss Blakemore, and Doctor
Hamilton put down his pen and removed his glasses.

"There's a woman to see you."

"Well?"

"The thing is—she's from over the Ranges. You've
never seen her before."

"So why is she here?" Doctor Hamilton stood up. "Miss Blakemore, what's happened? What's the trouble?"

"She's in a terrible state. I really can't manage her. Could you—could you possibly squeeze her in before Jack? You must have heard the noise in the waiting room."

He remembered vaguely a more than usual rumpus outside his door. He had put it down to children, as it usually was. "I'd better see her, then. Jack won't mind. But tell me more first. How did she get here? Drive herself? In that state? Why didn't she go to someone nearer?"

Miss Blakemore did her best to pull herself together. She brushed loose strands of hair off her forehead and blew her nose. "She was brought in. A couple of men I'd never seen came with her—said it was time someone did something about her and it wasn't really their responsibility but would the doctor see her. Then they went."

"Are they coming back?"

"They didn't say. I—I didn't think to ask. I don't know. I think, perhaps, they mightn't."

"So what do we do with the lady? If I don't put her in the hospital, how does she get home—wherever that is?"

Miss Blakemore had no answers. At that moment a voice from the waiting room shouted, "Miss Blakemore. Can you come? Quickly?" As she reached the door Doctor Hamilton said, "Bring her in," and went, himself, to the door.

"She's just fainted," a reproachful voice said as they opened the door.

They carried her in together and laid her on the examining table. She was not very heavy, nor very tall. She was still quite young—thirty-seven, perhaps. Her fair hair could have been pretty if someone had recently brushed it, and her face could have been beautiful if it were not for the exhausted shadows round the eyes and the hollows under the cheekbones. She wore jeans, a homemade pullover, and a windbreaker, all much worn and just now not very clean.

Doctor Hamilton bent over her. "She's coming round, I think. All right, Miss Blakemore, you'd better go and calm the waiting room down."

Her eyes had been open for some time—very wide, deep blue, and alarmed—when she made the first, classic remark. "Where am I?" She seemed to understand when he told her, but at once she tried to sit up. He put his hand on her shoulder.

"Don't try to get up for a few minutes."

"I have to. I think I must go to the police."

"You would do best to lie there while you tell me why you need to go to the police. And tell me how you came to be in my office." It took some time, and a pill that he assured her would do nothing but good, before she began to relax. When she started to talk her words came slowly and with a great effort. They appeared to make little sense.

On an impulse Doctor Hamilton said, "How long is it since you last spoke to anyone?"

After quite a long pause she said, "I think—twenty-four hours."

"Where do you live?"

She told him the name of a place he had heard of only vaguely. He knew only that it was a very small town in the rough country south of the dam. "Was it someone in town, then, that brought you in just now? Surely there was a hospital or a doctor's office nearer than mine?" Watching her eyes, he saw the earlier signs of panic creep into them again. "I don't mean," he said quickly, "that I'm doubting your word. I only wondered—whatever's worrying you, surely you could have talked to the people in the town? Why have you not spoken to anyone for twenty-four hours? And why were you brought here? Don't hurry. We'll get it all sorted out in time, and then we'll see about the police." The last word brought an instant reaction. She began to struggle to sit up. Again he put his hand on her shoulder. "Please don't worry. I know the police here. They'll send a man to talk to you if I phone them. Just lie there quietly and try to explain to me why you need the police." Under the insistent pressure on her shoulder she sank back again. Before she had begun to speak there was a knock at the door and Miss Blakemore beckoned him.

"I think I was just about to get some sense out of her," he said in an irritated whisper.

"I'm sorry, but I had to see you. One of the men who brought her in has come back. He wouldn't talk to me. He wants to talk to you. Can you see him?"

He looked over his shoulder. "I don't like to leave her, but—will you stay with her for a few minutes? Try to keep her talking. Try to get her to make sense. I suppose I'd better see this man."

He was middle-aged, obviously a farmer, and perplexed. "We didn't know what to do with her. She was in such a state. She looked so sick. We thought she'd collapse out there on the track. We was coming in this way, anyway. Simplest thing seemed to be to bring her to you. What's wrong with her, Doc? Any idea?"

"Not yet. I will in time. She's shocked, and I doubt if she's eaten for days. You'd better tell me all you know."

It turned out to be less than he had hoped. The farmer, Bob Plunket, was on his way to the railway to pick up some superphosphate. As there was also some for his neighbor they had come in together. Theirs were fairly isolated farms, tucked away among the hills, and there was a lot of dirt track before they met the gravel road, and even more of that before they came to the asphalt one. They had just turned onto the paved road when they saw her, miles from anywhere, as he explained. She was walking—tottering, rather—and they stopped to ask if she needed help. " 'Course she needed help. Trouble was would she take it. She was scared to death of us at first." Gradually they'd been able to reassure her. She wouldn't tell them what was wrong—only said she must get into town. "We didn't like to pry, see? So we reckoned the best thing was the doctor's place. By that time she was kind of hysterical. You saw, didn't you?"

"She wants to see the police. Any idea why?"

"Go on. She never said anything about that. Geez." He pushed his hat back and scratched his head. "What do you reckon? She in trouble?"

"I'm trying to find out. There's trouble all right there somewhere. It's got to be pretty big trouble. But I'd guess nothing criminal."

In the end Plunket left, leaving his address and telephone number. "Let us know. Anything we can do to help. Poor kid. I never seen anyone so—so kind of—in agony." It was a word he seldom used, and he brought it out awkwardly.

Doctor Hamilton went back to her then, leaving Miss Blakemore to pacify the waiting room once again. She was sitting up and he saw that Miss Blakemore had taken it upon herself to provide a cup of tea. She seemed better and her cheeks had become faintly pink. "So now—try to tell me why you want to see the police."

It took a long time in the telling because it was not easy to tell. And it came out in spurts and rushes separated by long silences. At first there was little coherence, but by degrees it fell into place well enough for him to pick up the telephone and ask if someone could come over from the police station.

"It'd be better if you went back with him and talked to them there. After that, I'd like to put you in the hospital for a few days." She became agitated at once. "Well, we'll see. Wait till you've told everything there is to tell. You must, you know, so they can help."

Afterward he learned from the police that her name was Frances Bellini. She was a widow. Already—at thirty-seven she was a widow. Her husband had emigrated from Italy, his one dream to have a farm of his own. Frances had married him at a time when she had begun to make a modest reputation as a singer—in fact it was her singing that had brought them together—and she was already making a small income. She gave up what she had begun to call her "career" in order to marry Tony, and with the money she had made she was able to contribute to the purchase of the farm. It had to be a small farm, it had to be inaccessible, and it had to be only moderately productive, otherwise they could not have afforded it. Tony had struggled with his conscience when she gave up her career. She told him she had no regrets, and if she had, the joy on Tony's face as they first drove in at their own boundary gate was sufficient for her to put up with any amount of hardship. She found she enjoyed the solitude and, like him, she rose to the almost overwhelming challenge the farm presented. After two years they had a daughter— Bianca because of her fair hair. Then, when Bianca was twelve, Tony's tractor overturned and he was killed. She was left with the choice of selling and returning to the city, or trying to carry on. They had just begun to show a small profit. At the time he died the season was good and the prospects were promising. Bianca begged her to stay.

Bianca still went to the local school, meeting the school bus where the gravel road ended, and on fine days leaving her pony in a yard near the road as the few other children did. On wet days Frances took her as far as the bus route in the pickup. Frances had faced the fact that soon Bianca would have to go away to high school and probably board in a bigger town. For the time being they were happy where they were. Besides, Frances had come to think of the farm as a kind of sacred trust left her by Tony. There had been none but the usual problems and disappointments of a farm until now.

At this point Frances had become incoherent. She had turned so white that she was given hot, sweet tea and told to rest awhile. She had continued at last, often recalling the past as well as the present. Time, it seemed, had become confused in her mind and she could not say how long ago it had all happened. She only knew too much—an eternity—of time had gone by since then.

3

Tony bought the piano at the first auction sale they went to, when they were trying to furnish the farmhouse as cheaply as they could. They had intended to buy a kitchen table, and there had been one listed in the advertisement for the sale. It was exactly what Frances wanted—the right size, strong and well-made. She found herself praying that it would not bring a higher price than they could afford. But Tony had seen a piano that had not been listed. He played a few notes on it; slightly out of tune, a little tinny; but he turned a brilliant face to Frances.

"Every house must have something to *play*."

Frances had said, "We can listen to the radio." But she knew from that moment that she had lost her kitchen table. It cost far less than a kitchen table would have but it was not much good for rolling pastry or chopping onions. But from the moment they eased it off the rear of the pickup and got it into the house Bianca was drawn to it as to a magnet. As soon as she was big enough she reached up with dirty, pudgy fingers and hit the notes one by one. Soon she was picking out tunes with fingers slightly longer, but still dirty. She hummed to herself as she did so, finding the note her voice had indicated.

Tony listened carefully to that high, thin humming and then said to Frances with great delight, "She has an ear."

After that he taught her the Italian songs he knew, and Frances sang nursery rhymes and old folk songs to her. Accompanying the songs, Frances found she did not regret the delayed arrival of their kitchen table. Then Tony decided Bianca must be taught to play the piano.

Frances looked at him in dismay. "How? How can we find a teacher here? How can we find the time and the money to *take* her to a teacher? How far would we have to go? Back to Sydney?"

Tony asked everyone if they knew where a music teacher might be found. Frances, saying nothing, wondered how the lessons would be paid for.

In the end it was the postmistress who solved the problem for them. She put them in touch with a neighbor they never knew they had—an old gentleman who lived with his wife in the house left to her by a farming uncle who had died without children. The old gentleman had once been a music inspector for the state government and now, living in these rural surroundings, missed his music and the people who made it. When they brought Bianca to him he willingly gave her a few preliminary tests and then, looking at them both with something like joy, said he would be glad to teach Bianca to play the piano and—no, he did not want payment. Teaching Bianca would be his hobby and his pleasure.

After that she went regularly to him, and because he told her pianists had to take care of their hands, the fingers she now carefully placed on the keyboard were never dirty again. But she forgot about them when she was outside helping her father or taking the dog rabbiting. Frances, watching her, hearing her singing in that high, true voice as she skinned and degutted the rabbits afterward, said nothing, and hoped her music teacher did not expect her to give up everything for her music.

One day in spring she came into the house giggling. "What's funny?" said Tony.

"Do you think I look like a bird, Daddy?"

He looked at her solemnly for a moment. Then he nodded. "Yes. Why have I not seen it before? You look just like one of our hens when she's broody. All fluffed feathers and a dreamy look."

She laughed with delight but shook her head. "Wrong. I think I look like a leatherhead bird. Other leatherheads think I do, anyway."

"Bianca!" Frances was reproachful.

But she looked at her mother with a glint in her eye. "This time it's true. I'm not making it up."

"You mostly are," said Frances dryly.

"But this time I'm not."

"Then tell us," said her father.

She told them how she had been standing under a tree down by the creek and had heard a leatherhead in the branches above, making his creaking, curious noise, and had mimicked him to such good effect that he had come swooping down, fluttering around her. "And when he found it was only me, he flew off in a hurry, making a quite different sound. So I made that, too, and suddenly all the birds were quiet." She stopped, looked at her father, and said, "Why? Daddy, why did they stop? I didn't want them to."

"Because you stopped making the leatherhead's love call and were giving the danger call," said Tony.

She clapped her hands over her mouth. "No! Not really?" Then she turned to her mother, rushing to her and clutching her hand. "Aren't I clever? Aren't I clever to talk the birds' language?"

"Moderately," said Frances. "Quite stupid people can be good mimics." But she smiled and hugged her daughter as she said it.

After that Bianca practiced her bird calls and taught herself to whistle to enlarge her repertoire. It was another dimension added to her isolated life.

Two good seasons in a row decided Tony to make a down payment on a tractor. "Don't do it, Tony," said Frances when he told her.

He was surprised. It was the first time she had not fallen in with his schemes with great enthusiasm. "Why not?" he said. She could not tell him. There was no reason that she could put into words. Objecting to what was obviously a good idea made no sense. She could only agree that it was a good idea and smile, knowing it was something he should not do. And it was not the money she was thinking of.

He bought the tractor. When he allowed Bianca to perch on it behind him, Frances concluded it was Bianca's safety that had been her subconscious fear. She could not—would not—stop him from taking her when Bianca's pleasure in it was so obvious and there seemed so little need for alarm. But she could not stop herself saying, "Be careful, Bianca. Be very careful. Hold on tight. Tony, be careful." And all the time it was to be not Bianca but Tony that the tractor killed when it turned over on a hillside.

He had been dragging logs from the timbered part of the farm to build up the supply of firewood before the winter came. "See," he said to Bianca, "now we can make use of all this wood we couldn't reach before. The tractor is paying for itself." He looked round and smiled at her, and did not see the jutting rock on the upper side of the track. The tractor turned over quite gently, so that Bianca had time to jump clear. She thought that Tony had jumped clear too, but when the dust settled and the clashing and banging stopped she saw that he was pinned in some way between the steering wheel and the metal seat. Even then he did not seem to her to be badly hurt. He looked up, saw her there half tangled in the scrub, safe, and called out to her. When she came stumbling across to him she could see no pain in his face, only, as she tried so hard to explain afterward to Frances, a strange bewilderment, as if he could not quite remember why he should be lying there unable to move. She could see nothing wrong with him and clutched at the hand he held out to her. She felt it close round her wrist.

"Can you get out, Daddy?" she asked him. She was shaking all over and her voice would not come properly, but even now it was not with undue concern for him.

Instead of answering he smiled and shook his head. She tried to release her hand so that she could try to pull him away from the tractor. But he would not let her go. "Sing to me," he said clearly. "Sit beside me and sing." She had no choice. She sat down and, against all likelihood, she sang. At first it was a small, quavering sound, but in a few moments, seeing the peace that flowed over his face, she gained confidence and her voice became steady. It was a simple, sentimental little German song that Tony often asked Frances to sing for him because it spoke of homesickness, of nostalgia, and of mothers and families left behind in far-off lands. They always knew when Frances sang that his thoughts were going back to Italy and all that he had left behind when he came so far to search for the farm he wanted above all else. As Bianca sang she tried to work out ways of moving him. He still appeared not to be in pain and she thought that if she could find a stick strong enough to lever the seat up a little he might be able to roll away. Growing up on a farm, she had learned to be practical. She looked about and saw a little way along the track a broken branch that might serve. When the song came to an end she tried again to loosen his fingers.

"Why are you in such a hurry to leave me?" he said, and held her more tightly.

"I want to get you out, Daddy, or go and get Mummy to help," she said. He looked queerly, she thought, into her face and said, "Your mother will not be strong enough, and no one else will be here in . . ." He somehow choked off what he had been going to say, and now said only, "Sing the song to me again."

She sat and sang the little song over and over again, and from time to time she tried to extricate her hand.

"No," he said each time, and each time his voice was fainter. "Just sing."

Afterward it seemed to her she had been sitting there for hours and hours, because the ground she was sitting on grew harder and harder, and for days after he was gone she bore the bruised marks of his fingers on her wrist, and seeing them there was the hardest thing of all. There came a time when, finishing the song yet again, she turned and looked into his face. She felt her heart leap, because now his eyes were shut and the skin of his cheeks had changed to the curious yellow color that a suntan does when there is no flow of blood beneath it. She began to shake again. Now, when she tried once more to free her hand she felt his fingers slacken, and she watched as his hand fell back onto the dusty ground.

Still trembling, still watching his face closely, she got to her feet. At first she stumbled because her muscles were stiff, but at last, stepping back away from the overturned tractor, she looked at him again, one last time. She saw now what she had been unable to see while she sat beside him—a dark, ruby-gleaming pool in a hollow underneath the tipped-up wheel against which he lay. She screamed and, still screaming, clambered to the track and began to run for home.

Frances's first feeling when she saw her daughter coming stumbling across the paddock was not, she remembered afterward, of surprise, or even of shock, but simply that now was the time to act, that, somehow, this was what she had been waiting for. She ran to Bianca and met her at the paddock gate. She took her arm and supported her into the house, and all Bianca could say was, "Daddy—Daddy."

"I know," said Frances calmly. "Can you tell me what happened?"

Bianca was clutching her now, burying her face in the folds of the old, worn-out pullover. "The tractor." Frances just caught the muffled words.

It seemed that everything Frances did then was done mechanically, without thought. Leaving Bianca in the kitchen with a cup of hot coffee, commanding her to stay there and drink it, she went to the telephone. After a few minutes, pale now, but with a face from which all expression had gone, she returned with an armful of blankets, one of which she wrapped round Bianca.

"Stay there," she said. "Stay there until they come, and then tell them where to go." She did not wait for an answer, but left the house and, with her arms full of blankets, began her long run down the track to find the tractor—and Tony.

Neither Frances nor Bianca could recall much of the next two days. It seemed to Frances then that only one thing was important—to shield Bianca from further shock if she could. She did not foresee the incident of the cat. And this was where she made the biggest mistake of all. It was the day the two men from the undertakers came to see her. It had been a frosty morning and one of them was wearing, not the customary sober black suit, but a sheepskin jacket. They were talking in the kitchen where it was warm, and Frances, wishing to spare Bianca, had sent her off earlier with the dog to check a distant boundary fence.

Bianca went off, the weight of responsibility heavy on her now that her mother was on her own to run the farm. That she was rather small to be asked to go so far did not occur to her. It had to be done and she would do it. But, what with the cool morning and the clear air, so that she could see a long way, it turned out to be less of an undertaking than Frances had reckoned on. Bianca returned, scarcely noticing the car outside the garden gate, and went into the yard to tie up the dog. The hilly walk had loosened a number of knots that had been tight inside her and for the first time since the accident she was relaxed—relaxed and vulnerable. The door of the shed was open and she crossed the yard to shut it. Before she did so she looked inside to make sure she was not shutting any of the hens inside. It was dark, and she stood for a moment until her eyes adjusted. Then, in one corner on a pile of empty sacks, she noticed two points of light.

"Puss," she said. "What are you doing there? Come on out, kitty."

But the cat did not come out and she walked toward the pile of sacks. The cat, she saw now, was sitting up with something hanging from its mouth. She peered and saw that it was a tiny, half-eaten kitten. Its own kitten. She ran from the shed—to the house—to her mother.

Frances had not finished with the undertakers and seeing Bianca in the doorway, against the light so that her face was only a darkness between her and the bright sunlight outside, she said more sharply than she should have, "Go away, Bianca. Go away for another few minutes, please. I'll come and fetch you when I want you."

"But it's the cat," said Bianca. "She's—"

"Go away. I don't want you in here." And Bianca missed the note of desperation and only heard the harsh rejection in her mother's voice.

It was after this that the nightmares began. Frances had rushed to bring her in as soon as the two men had left, had soothed and comforted her, and had thought that all was well. It was natural that she should put the nightmares down to Bianca's ordeal with her father. The cat eating its own kittens, horrible though it was, seemed a minor affair. She did not for a moment connect herself with the cat, both rejecting their young. But Bianca did—without being aware that she had. And the nightmares began.

They came regularly at eleven o'clock each night, just when Frances had begun to hope that this time they would not come. She would hear Bianca call out, not loudly, but with such urgency that every time she would drop everything and rush into Bianca's bedroom, to find her sitting bolt upright pointing at the wall opposite with staring eyes, saying, "Look! Look!" And there was nothing there to see. For Frances the worst part of these nightmares was that when she gently woke Bianca and the wide eyes began to focus, Bianca's first movement was to shrink back until her back was pressed against the bedhead. As Frances reached to take her in her arms, Bianca would stretch out her hands, palms forward, and sometimes she would whisper, "Go away."

It was always difficult to wake her and it was not until she was wide awake that Frances would ask, "Who did you think I was? Bianca, what were you afraid of?"

There was never a satisfactory answer. Sometimes Bianca would only say, "The cat—the cat. I thought—" and her voice would trail off, puzzled.

In the end it was Bianca's music teacher, Mr. Greville, who solved the problem. A small, ancient car stopped at the gate one day, and to Frances's surprise, Mr. Greville emerged from it. He had never visited them before, and she was pleased to see him, for she felt the need of a friend. When the opportunity came she told him about the nightmares. When she had finished he was silent for a few minutes. Then he said, "Why a cat?"

By this time she had recalled the incident in the shed. She had had the cat long since removed, having seen Bianca's revulsion from it, and she had almost forgotten it. Now she told Mr. Greville. He said, "Hm," and looked at her closely through his spectacles. At last he said, "You must realize Bianca is a very sensitive child. It is obvious when she plays the piano. Have you thought—forgive me—but have you thought of bringing her to me again? Of continuing her music lessons? You know it is a great pleasure to me. And I think she might find the music would help her, especially after—" He gave a small cough, putting his hand with careful deliberation over his mouth. "Especially after all she has been through."

It was a remedy that would never have occurred to Frances, but now, when she considered, she wondered why she had not thought of it before. And Bianca, though unable just yet to show enthusiasm for anything, proved ready enough to visit Mr. Greville again from time to time. And—yes, she would practice. Yes, she would work on her pieces again for him. It was a positive step in what Frances thought of as rehabilitation. And little by little she saw Bianca's pleasure in her music increase, and little by little the nightmares became fewer, and at last disappeared.

4

The time came when Mr. Greville asked if Bianca would like to take an examination. She was fourteen. She gasped, looked at her mother, and said, "Oh, could I, Mummy? Could I?"

"Is it necessary?" Frances asked. And Mr. Greville replied, "Not necessary unless she wants to make music her career."

"You think she could?" Frances was surprised. She had not taken the lessons so seriously, but after all, it would have been her own career. She looked at Bianca now and saw the shining expectancy in her face, waiting for a decision.

Mr. Greville replied cautiously, "It is possible. But it's early days for such a decision. To make it her career, even if she were good enough, would mean giving up everything else. It's a lot to ask, but there would be no harm in taking this exam now if she wants to."

There seemed innumerable obstacles, but he removed

them all. He filled in application forms, he drove her himself to the nearest town where she could sit for it, and he gave her all the moral and physical support she needed. But he did not promise her a pass. He only said she had as good a chance as anyone else. She would have to wait for the results.

So she waited, and Frances was surprised at the tension that was building up in her as time passed. Why it meant so much to her she did not know, but guessed it had something to do with being able to lay an achievement like this on Tony's memory.

It was the very morning of the impending disaster that the results came through. Mr. Greville telephoned to say he had just been to the post office and found there was an official letter there for Bianca and he was sure it contained the result of her examination. He knew there was no postal delivery along their mail route until the next day, and should he open the letter and read her the result?

Frances beckoned Bianca. "Well, would you rather wait, or shall Mr. Greville read it for you?" Bianca clasped her hands, gazed at the wall, and ceased to breathe. At last she said, "Ask him to read it."

There was a pause, and Frances could hear the rustle of paper tearing. She handed the receiver to Bianca. "Here. You listen."

Then Mr. Greville's voice came. "You've got a distinction. Well done, Bianca. Congratulations. I'll give the letter back to Mrs. Jones now and she'll send it out to you tomorrow."

The morning passed for them both in a kind of floating

dream. "Cloud nine," said Bianca happily. And for the first time since Tony died, Frances was truly happy.

It had been a sunny day, but there was going to be a frost, and Frances lit the fire early, while she could still see to gather sticks for kindling. The outside jobs for the day were done. She and Bianca together had been round the lambing ewes. They had taken bales of hay to the weaned calves and Bianca had said the grass had begun to grow and they would soon be able to stop feeding them. She had killed a sheep and hung it up—of all the jobs she had learned to do, the one she liked least. But it was done, and tomorrow she would cut up the mutton for the next few weeks. There remained only the daily household jobs. While she began to prepare the dinner Bianca went off to shut up the fowls and bring in the milker. As usual, she was humming as she went. The sun had just disappeared behind the hills.

Frances was bending over the sink, and later she remembered vividly that she was having the usual battle with slicing the squash for supper. She found it odd then that this was her most precise memory of that time. She heard a sound at the door and, without turning round, said, "How many eggs today?" It was a little odd that Bianca did not reply, but she went on, "I think I'd better get some more shellgrit next time we go into town. Put it on the list, will you, dear?"

It was then, because Bianca still had not replied, that she turned round. It was not Bianca who had come in. Two young men were walking from the door toward the table. Murmuring to one another, they were not aware that she had spoken. One of them wore a sheepskin jacket. At first she was not particularly alarmed.

It was rude, certainly, that they had come right into the kitchen without being asked. But she had already learned that country manners were free and easy. And it was not the first time people had got lost in the hills and had come to ask the way.

"Yes?" she said, and even smiled. Their next move surprised her. They sat down at the table and one said, "Got anything to eat?" She felt the first prick of fear then. It was a practical enough request, but the tone was not one of someone asking a favor. She was suddenly angry, and said, unwisely and too sharply, "Naturally there's food here, but I'm not accustomed to handing it out to people who speak to me like that." As soon as she had said it she knew it was her first mistake.

The youth who had spoken got up, pushing the chair back so that it shrieked across the floor. He was not tall, and he did not look particularly healthy, but there was no disguising the muscular frame. Whatever his activities were, they had made him too strong for her. He walked round the table and came and stood in front of her. She did not step back, but it took all her self-control to stay where she was. She was distinctly aware of his jeans, his studded belt, and his leather jacket. He was hot, and she could smell him. She said quietly and as evenly as she could manage, "I'd rather you left my house."

The youth who still sat at the table suddenly laughed.

The one who faced her only said, "I bet." Before she could move he grabbed her shoulders, spun her round, and said, "Go on now. Get us something to eat. We'll leave your house when we're good and ready."

She stumbled toward the sink and saw the knife she had been using for the squash. She clutched it. And then slowly let it go again. Even with the knife she could not take on two of them. She heard a movement behind her and turned. The one who had been at the table was now cruising round the cupboards, opening and shutting the doors.

"What are you looking for?"

She wished she had not said it, when he replied simply, "Money."

"I don't keep it there." It seemed a small triumph, but he circled the room, peering at cupboards and shelves as he came, and then, when he reached the sink, said, "Then where is it?" He was smaller than the other, but there was more intelligence in his face. Neither showed any emotion of any kind. They regarded her, she now saw, as a means to an end and nothing more. At that moment she knew they would take what they wanted and she could not stop them. They would take it—and go. And they would not go before that. She moved slowly to the stove.

"I'll get you food. And while you're eating I'll get you the money—all there is."

"OK." They went back to the table and sat down again. "But we'll come with you while you get the money. Where is it? Under the bed?" They found this funny and both laughed.

She took down the plates to warm, heated the stew, and

laid knives and forks on the table in front of them. She schooled herself to behave naturally and calmly. A show of fear, she somehow knew, would delight them. And she was terrified now, because as she moved about the kitchen a new thought had come to her. Very soon Bianca would come back, and she would walk in at the kitchen door just as they had done, and she would walk straight into unimaginable trouble. If they could eat and take the money and go before Bianca finished putting up the calf for the night. It was an effort not to seem hurried when something inside her was screaming, quickly! quickly!

They did not speak to her anymore. She was of no interest to them now while the food was on their plates. They bent their heads and ate, and they stopped only when the saucepan of stew was empty. They demanded dessert, and as she rummaged in the refrigerator for ice cream her brain was working feverishly. An excuse to go outside was what she needed, so that she could forestall Bianca and tell her to run away. She took a jug and went to the door. "I'm going to the dairy. You'll need milk."

But one of them had looked into the refrigerator when she had it open and had seen the milk there. He got up and went to the door. "You'll stay here with us. What's wrong with the milk here?" He pointed to the refrigerator.

"I'm not sure it hasn't soured." She had lost her chance. They would never let her go out now.

She thought they would never finish. She stood with her back to the stove, watching them. They looked so ordinary. They ate as if they were really hungry, but as anyone else would eat. Once she almost spoke. If she could just get through—reach their feelings. Everyone had feelings, so she believed. But, looking at their bent heads, she knew they had forgotten her already. She was not in their world. There was no point of contact, and anything she said or did would be ignored unless it got in their way. If it did, she would be brushed aside. And if she were broken as they brushed her aside it would be nothing to them. If Bianca came in now, and if she had anything they wanted, they would take it—and then brush her aside, too. As she pictured her daughter coming through the door, unknowing, she wondered if she could manage to kill them. But the shotgun was in the office and the cartridges were in a locked drawer. She had no other weapon.

At last they pushed their plates away and stood up. "Now—where's the money?"

All she had was in her handbag in the bedroom. The thought of their penetrating farther into the house and into her bedroom was insupportable. Her only—inadequate—thought was to lock the kitchen door that led to the rest of the house. "It's in my handbag. I'll get it." But the small one was too quick. He reached the door at the same time.

"I'll come."

She was facing him in the doorway, and behind her back she was trying to turn the key. But again he was too quick. "Oh, no," he said and would have reached behind her for the key. It was at that moment that, over his shoulder, she saw Bianca appear at the back door. She wiped all expression from her face, looked directly at him, and said, "It's the electrical fitting in the bathroom. I did telephone for you. Come this way."

Taken totally by surprise, he took a step back and she slipped away from him. She appeared, then, to see Bianca standing in the doorway.

"What do you think you're doing here? What are you doing in my house? I've told you to keep away. Go away at once. Go home. Don't you ever come here again." She was shouting, and there was a high, crazed note in her voice. She took a step forward as if she would attack the figure in the doorway.

Her deception worked. As quietly as she had come, Bianca melted away and the doorway stood empty. The two youths were looking at Frances with the only emotion they had so far shown, clear on their faces: sheer amazement.

The longer they looked at her the better. She began to babble. "See? She will come here. She's a neighbor's child. I shouldn't tell you this, but she's not quite—you know— and she's got some kind of disease. I have to keep her away because it's catching. Don't ask me what it is. I don't know, but the trouble! The trouble her parents take not to get in physical contact with her, you wouldn't believe. But they let her come here. It's criminal." Eventually the inspiration and the babble ran out and she stopped. They still looked at her and for the moment had no words.

No sound came from outside. While they had been eating, the night had come down and it was quite dark. There was only blackness in the doorway now. The larger of the two youths left the table and came toward her.

"Come on. Let's get the money. You show us."

The other youth, she saw, was looking at the empty doorway. He said, "Maybe we shouldn't have let her go."

She gave a kind of laugh. "You go then. You find her. And bring her back. And see what you get. Go on. Let's have her here. Let's ask her. Don't blame me for what happens afterward." It was the only approach that could have succeeded. The relief of seeing him turn back from the open door made her stagger. She put her hand on the sink for support.

The youth that stood beside her said, "Here, what's up? Come on. Get moving. If you're going to keel over you're going to give us the money first." He pushed her toward the door into the hall.

She did not keel over. Not then. Having wished them gone, her one aim now was to keep them as long as possible. It was only—a long time afterward as it seemed to her—when at last they began to be suspicious of her determined and inexplicable efforts to make them stay, that they left her, taking all her money and the keys of the pickup. And, as an afterthought, tearing out the telephone cord. She watched them walk out of the back door into the dark, and she heard them, after a time, start the pickup. And then she heard them drive away. She listened as the sound of the engine diminished, faded, and did not stop. She listened until it had quite died away. Then she waited. That half hour's waiting was worse than anything that had gone before. More than anything the youths had done, the picture that had been left in her mind of Bianca's face as she stood in the doorway was the worst penalty she paid that night. She sat at the table watching the clock, holding herself in as best she could. When the clock began to sway curiously on the wall she reached for a package of cookies and took up the knife she had thought of using on the young men. She slit open the package and tried to eat. Because she could not wait to boil the kettle she drank a mug of milk. At last the endless half hour was up. She picked up a flashlight, took a windbreaker off a hook on the back porch, and went out into the garden.

She thought at first that Bianca might be hiding in one of the sheds, the henhouse, or the cowshed. There was no telling what Bianca might have done. But she was not in any of the sheds. She was not in the henhouse, or the cowshed. Judging it now safe, Frances called, "Bianca!" All that happened was that she set the dog barking. It had barked, she now remembered, when Bianca had come back, and that must have told Bianca something, but how could she have expected what she found? Frances stood, wondering where she should look next. It did not matter that she no longer had transport. Bianca had no transport either, and wherever she had gone she had gone on foot. It was on foot that she would find her daughter.

She started off down the track. The pickup had gone down the track but she had not heard it stop. There was another bit of track through the paddocks that led eventually to the next property. It seemed likely that Bianca would go for help. Frances set off down the path, quickening her pace as she told herself that this was what Bianca would surely have done. The neighbor's farmhouse was some three miles away. She thought she knew the route well, but in the dark everything looked different. There were steep slopes where she had not expected them, and twists and turns she had no memory of at all. The flashlight was only just adequate to keep her on the path. She stopped often, sometimes to listen and sometimes because she had tripped and fallen over a root or a pothole the light had not revealed. She began to call again, and then waited, holding her breath, and it seemed as if the hills dividing her farm from the next echoed "Bianca" for a long time after she had stopped calling. When no answer came she stumbled on, up steep slopes, down into gullies. She longed for daylight and began to think it would never come.

How far could Bianca have gone, in the night, on foot? If she had not gone in this direction, which? There was not much choice. No tracks led anywhere on the eastern side of the farm but to paddock gates. There was nowhere to go but into another paddock. The boundary ended in rocky hillsides, the perimeter of the wildlife reserve. If Bianca had gone along the track to the road, they would have come upon her as they left. But Frances had listened carefully and would surely have heard if they had stopped. Bianca may have heard them coming and hidden until they passed. There was plenty of scrub on each side of the track. So she might still be going on toward the town.

At this point Frances sat down—and felt herself drown in a wave of exhaustion and hopelessness. She put her head between her knees and let her mind go blank. She came to herself again when she felt the flashlight slip out of her fingers and her forehead hit the ground as she rolled forward. She breathed in deeply and slowly, reached for the flashlight again, and with the help of a nearby low-hanging branch got to her feet. Perhaps the moment's collapse had pulled her into gear again. She knew now what she had to do. She had to reach the neighbor's farmhouse and if she had not found Bianca by then she must ask for help and ring the police. She walked on.

For perhaps a quarter of an hour she walked without stopping, flashing the light from side to side. The neighbor's house stood on a flat, surrounded by cleared paddocks, and she should have reached the flat by now. She stopped again and let the light play on the surrounding trees, behind, where she had come from, and as far ahead as it would reach. For the first time she noticed that the track seemed to have narrowed. It was no longer the two wheel marks she had started following and which, she knew, led to the next farm. Now she was on only one track and as she looked more carefully she realized that somewhere—but how far back?—she had veered onto a sheep path and she was no longer heading for the farm. For a moment despair forced her to rest, and she leaned, drooping, against the nearest tree.

In the end she pushed herself up and went on. The day must come soon and then, surely, she would know where she was. For a long time she did not look up. She walked with her mind elsewhere, almost numb and scarcely conscious, forcing herself on at a pace she was unaware was gradually getting slower and slower.

After an eternity of time something penetrated her sleeping mind. She woke to the realization that she had heard a bird call. It had been a brief, harsh, but hesitant sound—a sleepy sound. But it was a bird. Swept by a surge of relief, she looked up, searching for the coming day. And, looking up, she did not see the rock in her path and she fell, rolling helplessly down the slope. The flashlight flew out of her hand, hit a stone, and broke.

She seemed to fall endlessly, and the tops of trees whirled round her head and rocks and stones battered her. If she had been alert, awake, and fed, if fear and anxiety had not drained her of all energy, she might have stopped herself. Her will and muscles failed her and she gathered speed frighteningly until she felt herself roll over for the last time. Something terrifyingly cold engulfed her and she plunged into the headwaters of the dam. The cold and shock brought her to life. Automatically she struck out with arms and legs, brought herself to the bank, and, gasping, climbed out.

For a short time she was too cold to move. But she knew she must move before all movement became impossible. She got to her feet, swayed for a moment as the still tentative light of the new day grew black before her eyes, and took a deep breath. She regained her balance and her eyes began to see again. The dam spread out before her, still blanketed in moving wisps of fog. Here and there a darkening of the mist told her where the shoreline reached down to the water, or one of the small islands loomed ghostly through it. She turned again, saw the winding sheep track down which she had so precipitately come, and took her first wavering steps toward it. Before she reached the first steep pitch she turned back once more to look at the dam. From the east, glinting over the hilltops, the first shafts of sunlight pierced down through the fog and turned the still surface pink. One of the islands stood out sharply on the water. There was no sign of life anywhere.

As she began to climb again, a growing rush of sound filled the air all round her. With the first of the sunlight all the birds had wakened and were giving voice, dominating them all the clear song of a thrush in the springtime.

Her aim was still to reach the neighbor's farmhouse. But as she climbed and as the day grew brighter the beginnings of hope filtered through the nighttime gloom. What if Bianca had gone home, now that the day had come? At first it was no more than the briefest thought and she banished it at once. But it came back, and gradually it assumed the status of a possibility. She climbed on up the slope, stumbling over the rocks, slipping into the washaways, panting. At least the effort was keeping at bay the creeping cold from her wet clothes. The thought kept returning and at last she took out the repressed hope and looked at it squarely. She had no idea of how she, herself, had looked during those minutes when Bianca stood in the doorway. It was the look on Bianca's face she remembered and which had driven her on all through the long night. So now she knew that first of all she must go home again.

She was tiring when she reached the place where she had

fallen. But she found the flashlight with its glass and bulb shattered, and picked it up, somehow encouraged. From now on she concentrated on the sheep track. Then, coming round the base of a big whitebox eucalypt, she saw the two wheel tracks. The sheep path had merged with the track on the right, going off at an angle, and was easy to mistake by flashlight. She was no longer lost, and her pace quickened.

When she reached the horse-paddock gate she had to lean against it for a time. There was now only the width of the paddock, the yards, and the small garden before she reached the door of her house. As she stood, her chest heaving, she tried to see if there were signs of life about the yards. Had the fowls been let out? Was the dog off its chain? Was the milker reunited with its calf? She could see nothing, and decided she was still too far away. Pushing herself upright she took the chain off the gate and went through.

She could see no movement as she got closer, but she could hear the cow protesting and knew the calf was still shut up. Perhaps Bianca had been too tired to do the milking. Very likely. But there was no sign of the dog, or of the fowls. When she went through the yards and up to the garden gate she could see that the back door was shut. She tried to remember if she had shut it when she went out. Most likely in her agitation she had left it open. Bianca must be at home, asleep. She almost ran up the path, falling in at the back door and calling, "Bianca! Bianca!" The house was quiet and the kitchen was cold. There had been no one at the stove since she left. Still with fierce hope she went through to Bianca's room, sure that she would find her asleep, probably still dressed with her shoes on the bedcover. Afterward she marveled that she had felt a momentary flick of annoyance.

But the room was empty. The bed had not been slept in, and the silence of the house mocked her. And now, at last, she collapsed on Bianca's bed and passed from a momentary unconsciousness into sleep.

She slept through all the hours of daylight, and woke at last when the increasingly desperate bellowing of the cow penetrated her sleeping mind. She woke slowly and unwillingly, instinctively drawing back from the situation to be faced. And she was still tired. When she opened her eyes the first thing that registered was that the window had moved. She shut her eyes and opened them again. The window was still in the wrong place. Slowly and painfully she sat up, and saw that she was in Bianca's bedroom and, inexplicably, not in her own. And it was her own shoes that were on the bedcover. With a rush her memory returned, and the shock made her fall back with her hands over her face. When she sat up the second time her mind had begun to race.

She found it confusing that the room was almost dark, and she looked at her watch. She had to get off the bed and turn on the light before she could read it. It said five-thirty. Morning? Or evening? In sudden panic she rushed into the kitchen and turned on the radio. After ten interminable minutes it told her it was evening. She knew then that she had slept all through the day. She should have been out, looking for Bianca, asking for help. But she had slept all day. Suddenly her legs gave way, she collapsed

onto the kitchen chair, and, with her head on her crossed
arms on the kitchen table, burst into tears.

Once again it was the bellowing of the cow that made
her move. She got up, and knew that she felt better and
able to cope afresh with whatever lay ahead. While she
made up her mind she did what immediately needed to be
done. It was too late to feed the fowls. They had all gone
to bed. But she fed the dog and let him off. She needed his
company now. Perhaps she should milk the cow, but instead she let out the calf, saying quite savagely, "At least
you can have *your* child."

Her first thought was to leave at once, but she had no
clear notion of where she might be going. What she needed
was transport and a telephone.

Remembering the young men she went round the house
locking doors and windows—something she and Bianca
ordinarily never bothered to do. It was not until she stood
ready to go, and with the key about to turn in the lock of
the kitchen door, that she suddenly pictured Bianca returning in the night, trying to get in—and unable to get
in. She pulled the key out of the lock and stood quite still
for a few minutes. Where else would Bianca go but home?
She would come tonight, and there would be no one there
and she would not be able to get in. Frances opened the
door again and went in, throwing her jacket on the table.
Then she went round the house turning on all the lights
and flinging back the curtains.

Then she sat down to wait.

It was an even longer night than the one before. Dawn
found her gaunt and dark-eyed. When she saw the first of

the light she gave up pacing through the house, snatched up her jacket again, and went out, this time leaving everything open. She remembered that she had let the dog off, and whistled for it. But it did not come, and she went on alone.

The sun had been up for some time when she reached the highway, and it was here, standing swaying in the middle of the road, that the two farmers had found her. As soon as they approached her she became hysterical and, thinking her gabbled account of loss and threat and helplessness too confused to be treated seriously, they decided that a doctor was what she needed. As she was sobbing and catching her breath quite helplessly all the way in, they had learned nothing further. If she had remembered to tell them her name they might have found out more, for they knew of Tony and the farm. But since his death she had preferred to live alone with her daughter and they had no opportunity of getting to know her. So they thought she was quite unknown to them and had, perhaps, been dropped from some passing car after a family row. It had been known to happen. Later, when they were told of the stolen pickup they told the local constable and began looking for it themselves. In the end they found it, for it had been abandoned within walking distance of a railway station.

5

By the time Hubert, Emily, and Paul reached home—in the dusk of a clear, mistless afternoon—their father had dealt with a suspected case of typhoid and a particularly messy car accident at one of the more hazardous nearby cross-roads, and his thoughts had long ago left the problems of the hysterical woman he now assumed safe in the local hospital. In any case, he was not in the habit of discussing patients with his family. So some time elapsed before they heard of her existence.

They trailed into the kitchen, dumping the picnic bas-kets and the empty drink bottles on the table. Their mother—large, placid, and gentle-faced—stepped back from the stove, a dripping wooden spoon in her hand.

"Would you mind removing those things from where I'm trying to assemble a filling and palatable meal for to-night? Hubert, put all the dirty things on the sink. Emily, take the baskets into the laundry where they belong. Paul, why are your clothes looking so extraordinary, and where are your glasses?"

"He fell into the dam," said Emily, emptying the baskets by the quick and simple method of tipping them upside down over the table. A few bits of dead grass and a twig or so fell on top of an unprotected cheesecake.

"Oh boy!" said Hubert, reached himself a knife from the rack, and quickly cut a slice from the cake.

"So you've had your dessert," said his mother. "Why can you never wait until dinnertime?"

"I'm always hungry," said Hubert. "That's why. And you always leave the dessert exposed."

"In future I shall lock it in the cupboard. Put the knife down, Hubert." She was still looking at Paul's clothes.

"I'll bet he's taken my piece," said Emily. "The bit with the biggest strawberry."

"Don't be silly," said Hubert, chewing noisily. "You know the biggest strawberry always goes to Paul—if we don't get it first."

Mrs. Hamilton had returned to the stove. "Now see what you've done. The white sauce has gone lumpy. And I still want to know why Paul fell into the dam and where his glasses are."

"Obviously," said Hubert, "his glasses are now in the dam."

"We did look," said Emily quickly. "But see, Mum, the water was all muddy from getting Paul out. They'd be there somewhere," she added hopefully.

"You really shouldn't let your brother fall into the dam. You know he's only *learning* to dog paddle." Mrs. Hamilton's shoulders heaved rhythmically as she stirred the white sauce with great energy.

"As far as I'm concerned," said Hubert, "he won't have the chance to fall into the dam again. I shan't be taking him again." A loud, wordless sound came from Paul, expressing strong indignation.

"Shut up, Paul," said Emily. "You know it was your own fault."

"I was looking for ducklings," he shouted.

"Did you see any?" Mrs. Hamilton turned from the stove, interested at once.

Emily and Paul told her simultaneously of the mother duck and the family of ducklings they had seen. Hubert quietly cut himself a second piece of cheesecake. By the time the description had come to an end, dinner was ready and Doctor Hamilton had poked his head around the door to say his office hours were finished. There was a sudden scurry to get Paul changed and the picnic things out of the way. Dinner was interrupted by several telephone calls and by the end of it Paul was sneezing and shivering.

"There. You see?" said Mrs. Hamilton. "He's caught a cold from being in those wet clothes. Put him to bed, Emily."

"We tried to dry the pullovers," said Emily as she pushed her brother through the door. "I thought it was better to have wet clothes on than be *naked.*" Outraged virtue seemed to ooze from her retreating back.

So nothing was said that night about the girl in the rowboat. The next morning Mrs. Hamilton said, "If you wouldn't mind, Hubert, I think it would be a good idea if you and Emily went back to the dam to have another look for Paul's spectacles. I can do without the car today. With any luck the water will have cleared by now. I shouldn't think you need take lunch again."

"Oh lord," said Hubert. "I had other plans."

"No doubt. But they can wait, and today might be the last chance for the glasses. It's Sunday, after all."

As they drove out, this time without Paul, who was confined to bed, Emily said, "We never told them about that girl."

"Why should we? Besides—" Hubert frowned, carefully negotiating a pothole, and said, "I'm not even sure there was a girl."

"Don't be silly, Hubert. We *saw* her."

"You said you did. I can't really be sure. I must say, I keep asking myself. It was a pretty heavy mist, you know. Anyway, there was no point in making a thing of it. A bit of non-news if ever I heard one."

"Maybe we'll see her today. Look out, Hubert. That was a sheep you nearly hit."

The morning was clear, shining, and calm, like the morning before. They reached the dam, left the car where they had left it before, and walked along the shore. The water was dazzling in its still brightness. From across it came the sound of a circular saw. And somewhere someone was mustering sheep. They could hear the dogs barking and the bleating of the sheep and occasionally the shout of a man.

"Working on Sunday?" said Hubert.

"Being a farmer means working any old day. You know that."

"I forgot. Glad I'm going to be a doctor."

"Doctors work any old day, too."

"Oh, hell."

"Think of the money, Hubert."

After a while Emily stopped. "Wasn't it here?"

Hubert had been walking with his head in the air, weighing the pros and cons of a medical career. Now he stopped. "I remember I could see the farm over there on that little promontory, and that little island with the scrub on it."

"Look down, Hubert. Where your feet are. That's where he fell in. I think it's here."

"OK. We might as well look here as anywhere. Wait till I get a stick."

"You don't want a stick. You'll only stir up the mud. Lie on your stomach and look into the water. That's what I'm going to do."

"If you say so, Emily." They lay side by side and for a time there was no sound but of wood being cut and the mustering. "It is curious, Emily, that those little wriggling, squirming things in the water are probably the beginnings of us. I find it humiliating. But the scientists may be wrong. We may have come down as seeds in a cloud of star dust from some remote galaxy. I should much prefer that, actually."

"Hubert, are you looking for the glasses? What's that bit of shiny stuff over there near where your hand is?" He looked, grunted, and gingerly slid his hand into the water.

"Hm," he said at last, and pulled his hand out. There was a swirl of mud and Paul's spectacles came out of the primeval ooze.

"They were there all the time. You see, you never *look.* "

"Don't you start. That's what Mum's always saying. Can't think why. I look a great deal."

"Not at the right things, Hubert. And then you're usually thinking of something else."

They sat back. Emily took the glasses from him and rinsed them. They appeared to be unharmed. "We can go back now," she said.

But they did not go back. The sun was warm, the view pleasant, and the grass reasonably soft and not very damp. They sat and looked at the dam. At first nothing moved. Then a small piece of the island detached itself and floated off quite slowly. Emily said, "A bit's come off the island."

"I know," said Hubert. "I've been watching it."

It was only a black speck and it seemed to be floating in their direction. After a while Emily said, "You see, Hubert, it *was* a boat. And that's the girl in it again. You did see it after all."

"I must have. But, Emily, am I seeing it now? Can you be sure you're seeing it? There may be a heat haze on the water."

"Hubert, it is a rather small girl in a rowboat, rowing in this direction. At ten o'clock on a spring morning there is no heat haze."

"If you say so, Emily." But as she was about to get up, he said, "Wait. Let's see what she does. She may be real, but she's pretty odd, you must admit."

Now they could see the ripples made by the moving boat on the mirrorlike surface as she rowed toward them. The ripples spread out soundlessly under the wide sky and she rowed on, cutting the surface in two, and gradually came nearer.

"She hasn't seen us," said Emily.

"She'll turn round to look where she's going in a minute and then she will. Emily, lie down the way we were before and don't move."

"Why should we? She's not a mother duck." Emily sat bolt upright to preserve her independence.

"Because if you remember when she saw us last time she disappeared so fast I really did think I hadn't seen her at all. We seemed to have frightened the life out of her."

"I can't think why. You look harmless enough, Hubert."

Hubert looked at her silently for a moment. She still sat with a rigid backbone and a slightly protruding jaw. "I can't say the same of you," he said at last.

She took a breath through expanded nostrils. Hubert hastily said, "Shsh!" and put a finger against his lips. Her lungs slowly emptied themselves. Hubert stretched out on his stomach facing the water. After a moment more of silent protest she did the same.

The little boat was very near now. They could hear the splash of oars and they could see the drops fall from the blades as the girl lifted them from the water. Very soon she would have to look round. They saw again the fair hair that covered her shoulders. Its sleek look had gone. There seemed to be twigs and bits of leaf tangled in it.

"She's a mess," whispered Emily.

"Wait," whispered Hubert and put his hand on her arm.

At last the girl looked over her shoulder, but they were directly behind her, flat on the grass and motionless, and she did not see them. She reached forward, slid the blades into the water, and took one long last pull at the oars. Then she shipped them and twisted round to put her hand against the bank. Now Hubert stood up. "I'll help you." He thought he had spoken quite quietly, quite gently, but the girl froze and on the pale face came a look of shock and horror. "It's all right," he said. "I just thought I'd give you a hand." And he held his hand out toward her.

Her mouth fell open and he wondered if she was going to scream. But no sound came. Instead she bent forward and pushed at the bank with all her might and the little boat floated out again into deeper water. They saw her settle herself and reach for the oars and in a moment the boat swung round and she was rowing frantically, hitting the water each time with a splash and lifting the oars again, sending showers of bubbles in all directions. As she rowed away they had their first clear look at her. She was thin as well as small, but the most noticeable thing about her was the gaunt expression of her face.

They watched in silence until she was out of earshot. Then Emily said, "I wasn't that much interested in her before. But now I am. Now I'm going to find out who she is. She looks quite bonkers to me."

For a long time Hubert said nothing at all. He had sat back on the grass again and now, with his arms round his legs and his chin on his knees, he watched the boat getting smaller and smaller as it crossed the dam, heading for the scrubby little island in the middle distance. It seemed he had not heard what Emily said, for presently he spoke, and his words surprised her. "She's needing help, and I'd give it to her, but how do we start?"

"We could feed her," said Emily.

"You think that's all? You think she's hungry?" The practical suggestion seemed to stun Hubert.

"I think she's crazy. But she might be less crazy if she were fed."

"How do we do that? She won't let us near her." It was a question for which they had no immediate answer. They watched as the boat receded. It was headed for the island and after a time the black dot it had become merged with the black dot that was the island and they did not see it again. "Do you think she lives there?" said Hubert as if his thoughts had traveled a very long distance since he last spoke.

"No one could live on an island that size, Hubert."

"She came from there and she's gone back there. Emily, how about hiring a boat and going to have a look?" He sprang up as if the thought had filled him with sudden energy.

"It's miles round to the boat shed and I haven't any money. Have you?" Emily looked at him as if he, too, were about to give cause for serious concern.

He felt in his pockets. When he had felt in them three times and produced a very clean handkerchief, a very dirty handkerchief, a cough drop, a button, and a box of matches, he shook his head. He stood for a moment, his eyes screwed up in the sunlight and fixed on the distant island. Then he said, "I'll look in the car. Mum often has some money tucked away somewhere." He was gone before Emily had time to speak—if she had intended to speak. But she had no such intention. For the moment there were no words for the baffled thoughts that were floating through her mind. She was accustomed to Hubert's normal behavior. He was not given to snap decisions, but now he was acting before his decision, snapped or otherwise, had really been reached. Not like Hubert at all. She waited, hoping there would be no money in the car.

He seemed to have been gone a long time, and she began to wonder if he had been struck by some other uncharacteristic impulse when his voice just behind her said, "Really, you'd never imagine the places Mum thinks of to hide money away. I found this in four different places—in the road map in the glove compartment, stuck behind the sun visor, under the driver's seat, and in the trunk under the spare wheel. It's my belief she'd forgotton most of them." He came and sat beside her, holding a bunch of bills under her nose. "Look. A king's ransom."

"Have you counted it?" It looked more like a posy he was offering her than the coin of the realm. There could have been a lot or a little.

"Give me a chance." He laid the bills on the ground between them and a small gust of wind immediately took two ten-dollar bills and sent them floating off into the dam.

"There," said Emily. "Now your other mother's got them. Are you satisfied?"

"Emily, what are you saying?" Hubert looked dazed.

"You're always raving on about water being your first

mother. Now she's taken the money. Better get it back before she swallows it." It had gone beyond arm's reach and Hubert had to step into the water to rescue it.

"There are times when I find you impossible, Emily," he said as he poured water out of his shoe.

She was looking smug, and only said, "Now you know what I have to put up with. Even if you are older, you can be impossible, too."

They counted out thirty dry dollars and twenty wet ones. "It's enough," said Hubert.

"It'll take us all day and we didn't bring any lunch. Have we enough for lunch, too?"

Hubert looked at her reproachfully. "Emily, this is an errand of mercy. We shouldn't be thinking about food."

"Well, I am. I hate being hungry. Besides, Hubert, have you thought—its Mum's money. It's like stealing."

"I have to tell you again, Emily, that this is an errand of mercy—what the reporters call a mercy dash. We're dashing to that island on an errand of mercy. I keep telling you."

"If you ask me, she doesn't want to be rescued."

Hubert was picking up the bills. He stopped now and sat motionless, his head still bent over the money. At last he said very quietly and without lifting his head, "I know she does. In spite of appearances, I know she does, and I'm going to find out what the trouble is. You can't stop me, Emily."

She knew when to stop arguing with Hubert. She got to her feet. "In that case I'd better come with you. And we'd better make a start."

It took them three quarters of an hour, driving in silence, to reach the boat shed. It was necessary to follow all the convolutions of the rugged shoreline, sometimes along the edge of the water, past small, struggling farms, sometimes, twisting and turning, up and over steep hills among the trees of the Nature Reserve, and at last along a well-made road that led to the dam wall. The sun shone down, calm and benign, not yet the ruthless, burning dehydrator of the summer months. And everywhere green spears were bursting out of the ground and sap was rising. It was midday when they turned off the paved road and arrived at the boat shed. Hubert turned off the engine and sprang out. He had vanished round the corner of the building before Emily collected herself and the ignition key and got out after him. She noted with a curious hollow feeling that the food stand was not open.

The reason was made plain when Hubert came bounding back saying, "Look, Emily, it's too early in the season for boats with outboards. They're all being serviced, but we can have a rowboat. Come on."

"The food stand, too, I suppose?" Her voice was faint.

"Of course. Come on. Hurry up, Emily."

She was still trying to think of reasons why they should not be here—why they should be heading for home—as they pulled out from the jetty. She knew they were expected home for lunch, she thought it possible their mother might want the car in the afternoon, although she had not said so. For one reason or another, sitting in a rowboat on the dam was where they should not be. But to Hubert their purpose was clear and was overriding all other considerations. He was needed. He had to go. The girl's face haunted him. The fear, the hunger (though for what?), the hopelessness had so worked on his imagination that he was, for the moment, obsessed. He rowed furiously, his face set, and stared unseeing at Emily as the boat leaped through the water in a series of surges.

"It's a long way up the dam," said Emily. "You'll never keep up that pace. You'll have flaked out before we're halfway there."

He grunted and rowed on, but the pace slackened a little and they proceeded rather more smoothly. The sun was well beyond the meridian when Hubert collapsed on his oars with bowed head and heaving chest. They were still less than halfway up the dam. Somewhere, still a long way ahead, was the island, if they could only find it, and the girl with the terrified face.

"Mercy dash," said Emily.

6

It had still been daylight when Bianca set off to find the milker. But now that the sun had set, the gullies and hollows had begun to gather the sharp air that already threatened frost. She stood at the gate looking down the long slope that led to the creek that watered the paddock. There was no sign of the cow, but she often visited the creek for her last drink of the day. She was probably among the willows that lined its course. And Bianca suddenly spread her arms and began to run down the slope. Today she felt that at any moment the joy inside her would rise up and suffocate her. It was not only knowing she had succeeded in the music competition; even more it was the confirmation that she could compete in an open field. And it was the sight of her mother's face—happy as she had not seen it since Tony died. All this was almost too much for one person in one day.

The dog raced ahead. His life was punctuated by Bianca's bursts of exhilaration. It was a long slope and at the end of it Bianca leaned, panting, against the first willow she came to. She could see the creek gleaming in the last of the daylight through the bare branches. In the distance it was already possible to see a haze of green among the willows, but now, close up, the first tiny leaves were scarcely visible. It was very still by the creek. It was too early in the year for frogs, and the birds, tonight, seemed to have settled early, perhaps aware of the frost to come. Only the small sound of running water hung on the quiet air.

When she had caught her breath she looked for the cow. She was nowhere to be seen. Sometimes Bianca thought she hid deliberately, not wanting to be parted from her calf for the night. But Bianca knew all the hiding places and she quite enjoyed the nightly game of hide and seek. She went first upstream, stepping over willow roots and brushing the long branches aside. The dog disappeared ahead, and returned after ten minutes or so to tell her the cow was not there. She patted him.

"I'll go just the same," she said. "You're not always right."

By the time she reached the first hiding place below a bluff of rocks that pushed the creek in a swirling curve, the gleam had gone from the water and there was very little daylight left. She turned back downstream, and once again the dog raced ahead. Its airily waving tail seemed to say, "I told you so." It did not worry her that soon darkness would come. Her only concern was to be out from among the willow roots while she was still able to see them, because of the mist that could quite suddenly come down after sunset. She had more than once lost her way in the mist, and she had learned to be frightened of it, as she was not of anything else that she had experienced in her fourteen years of life. So now, although she began to hurry a little, she also began to sing to herself—a gentle little song she had learned from her father. It was the only sound in the darkness that began to gather all about her.

She passed the track that had brought her to the creek and went on down, knowing now where she would find the cow—at the farthest point in the paddock. When Bianca heard her moo—unalarmed, but mildly protesting—she knew the dog had found her. By the time she came upon her, the creature was already making her way back up the creek. The dog followed behind, ignoring the attempts of the small red calf to play with him. The dog was old and had seen many calves come and go, and games no longer appealed when he knew from long experience that his dinner did not come until the calf was shut up.

By the time they came out from under the willows and began the long climb to the homestead, the night had come and frost was everywhere in the air. Usually at this point, if the wind was in the right direction, Bianca would begin to smell the burning twigs and dry leaves that her mother had kindled for the nighttime fire. It was a smell that always sent a kind of satisfied thrill through her for it meant another of the long, companionable evenings by the fire that were one of her winter pleasures. The sense of being shut in with her mother from the cold and some-times windy and wet nights, knowing the fowls were safe from foxes, the calf under cover, and the dog asleep in his hollow tree trunk never failed to please her. She never wished for anything else and hoped, when she thought of it at all, that the life they were leading might go on forever. School she enjoyed, and got on well enough with the other children, but many of their interests were foreign to her, as hers were to them, and she was always pleased when she got off the bus, saddled up her pony, and rode off down the track, knowing that for the next twelve hours she would see no one but her mother. That it was a curious existence for a girl of her age never crossed her mind. It was her existence, inevitable, right, and as she and her mother wished it. Tonight, with all the morning's news waiting to be taken out and savored all over again, and her mother's joy in it as great as her own, it would be a very special evening indeed.

She hurried past the cow to open the gate, let her through, and shut the gate behind her. The cow wandered on toward the shed where the calf would spend the night. Outside the shed door she stopped, looked round, and mooed gently. The calf dived underneath her for a final drink.

"In you go," said Bianca. "You've had all day to drink. It's our turn now."

With a loud sucking noise the calf removed his milky muzzle from under the cow and, encouraged by the dog, cantered in through the door. Bianca shut it. "There. See you in the morning." Then she went to shut up the fowls. It was too dark now to feed them. They would have to wait until the morning, too. From their perches they made sleepily indignant noises while she collected the eggs. She tied the dog up next, threw him a handful of dry food, and promised bones tomorrow. "When we cut up the sheep," she explained carefully.

Then she walked toward the house.

The back door was open, throwing a shaft of light across the last remaining cauliflowers in the vegetable garden. It would be cold in the kitchen with the door open, and she wondered why her mother had not shut it. She put the eggs in the meathouse and walked toward the door. She heard voices and assumed it was later than she thought and her mother had turned on the news.

So she stepped, unsuspecting, into the kitchen doorway. She was surprised, but not yet frightened, when she saw the two young men in the kitchen. She thought at first they must have lost their way, forgetting that she had seen no vehicle outside the gate. It was when she saw the sheepskin jacket that time suddenly stood still, fled backward, and she was standing again trying to tell Frances about the cat. At that moment she was balanced precariously on a mental peak, one side of which fell to black depths, the other to the daylit present and stability. It was Frances who tipped the balance, Frances who now offered her own safety for Bianca's, and whose expression as she caught sight of Bianca in the doorway suddenly changed, and Bianca saw again, but now intensified, only hostility in her mother's face. The suddenly screaming voice hit her ears like a blow. It took Bianca a moment to understand that she was being rejected for a second time, that the one person in whom she had learned to have total faith had turned against her, and that on this day of all days the only person who now mattered in her life had turned into a hostile stranger. In that first moment all she felt was bewilderment and a great confusion in her mind. After that came the knowledge that she was alone and that there was now no one she could turn to. And she thought only of escape. She turned and ran—away from the house, out of the garden, the yard, through the gate, and down into the paddock. Not once did she think of using the track—or any track. Escape lay where no one went and where no one could find her. She ran. And she did not stop running until the house and all that it contained were out of sight and out of hearing. It was only then that she stopped. She had no idea where, or how far she had run, but when she regained her breath she ran on—away from houses, people, anything that connected her with the life she had always led. Although she was not aware of it, she was going downhill, always downhill. When she came to a fence she climbed over it. When she came to a creek she crossed it or went along its downhill course. She passed the boundary of their own farm without noticing. She ran on—away. That was the only thought in her head at that time.

Once or twice she changed direction because she thought she saw lights in the distance. Now she was frightened of people—any people. She might have stumbled on all through the night if she had not suddenly found herself at the edge of a great stretch of water. If she had been running as she had run at first, she would have gone right into it, for her thoughts were not for what lay ahead, but only for the unbelievable thing she had left behind. But she was no longer running. She was shambling now at no more than walking pace, driven forward only by desperation.

So she stopped at last, bewildered, and for a little while no thoughts came at all to tell her what she should do next.

It took her a long time to realize that she had somehow come to the bank of the big dam. She had no idea how. She looked at the gleaming ebony of the water, stretching away into an impenetrable blackness. It was very calm, unruffled, and to her as she was at present, welcoming. As she stood there some of the dreadful tension that had driven her onward began to slacken. She swallowed and felt her throat muscles loosen and her breath grow steady. She began to feel, too, an overwhelming weariness. Out on that wide blackness was sleep, and to sleep would mean forgetting everything. These notions came to her one by one, and slowly, as her body felt the pull of that waiting oblivion. If the power of movement had not momentarily left her she might have stepped out into the quietly waiting depths. But before she felt able to move again another thought came to her. One of the neighbors who lived on the edge of the dam kept a boat in a small, unlocked boat shed. She began to make her way along the edge of the dam.

She seemed to be walking forever, often falling and coming across obstacles that had to be clambered over, or around, or under. Occasionally, sudden scuffles, a snort in the darkness, or blundering footsteps would tell her she had disturbed some animal of the night, or a sleeping horse or steer. But she reached the boat shed at last and sat down to think once more. She might have sat beside it indefinitely if she had not suddenly felt a change in the night. For the first time she looked about and began to take in her surroundings. The day was on the point of breaking, and soon, if she did not take the boat now—at once—she would be visible to anyone who might be looking out across the waters of the dam. And she knew, without thought, that during the daylight hours she must remain hidden. When she finally slid the boat into the water, climbed in, and pushed herself off, she still had no firm idea of where she would go. Her mind was still fixed on escape and nothing else.

It was not the first time she had rowed a boat. Her father had owned one, which they sold when he died. With confidence she fixed the oarlocks and adjusted the oars. She took the first few long strokes, and the boat glided out, away from the shore and into the steel-gray water. In the early dawn she was still no more than a darker shadow on the dark surface, but before long, when the sun came over the hills and threw her shadow across the water, she would be very visible. She rowed on blindly, and it was only by chance that she looked up, scarcely seeing what surrounded her, but registering almost subconsciously that she had rowed past a small island. After a time she stopped rowing, holding the oars with dripping blades while the boat glided on until momentum ceased and it hung motionless over the depths while the ripples it had made gradually spread out, thinned, and faded. The island was now directly behind and she saw that it was covered with scrub and one or two small trees. At the water's edge there were rushes. It was a very small island, but the boat could be concealed and so could she. She bent forward, dipped the oars into the water again, and turned the boat.

By the time the sun came up there was no longer any sign of Bianca or the little boat. And the ripples of its passing had already died away. The sun climbed slowly from behind the hills and shone down on the dam. And gradually the business of the day began. Daytime sounds floated out across the water, birds flew, combustion engines throbbed among the distant hills. Men moved out from their houses and one woman, far away, came down to the water's edge, stood for a time, and then turned back.

Bianca, beneath the shelter of the scrub that covered the island, was asleep. And the boat was deep in the rushes, tied to a small tree, and hidden from any part of the dam. She slept all day and did not notice when the sun began its westering course, or when the first of the mist began to form with the coming of the drop in temperature. When she woke, no longer in sunshine, the mist had thickened. She lay for a long time with open eyes, seeing nothing but the small leaves and twigs that sheltered her. There was no sky. There was no water, or land. Except for the twigs and leaves there was nothing. At first she did not even ask herself where she was. She knew only that she was hungry, thirsty, and cold. After a long time she tried to stand up. She tried twice and each time her knees collapsed and she found herself back under the bushes. The third time, holding onto the tree the boat was tied to, she managed to stand upright. Her legs trembled and her head swam for a few minutes, but she clung to the trunk and after a time the dizziness passed. She leaned against the tree and looked about. There was nothing to be seen at all. There was no movement of air. There was no sound. She tried to remember where she was and what she had been doing before she so unaccountably went to sleep among these bushes. Her memory told her nothing. She looked down at her jeans and her shoes. Both were torn and very dirty, but nothing about them told her how they had come to be so. She put her hand up to her head and felt the long, tangled hair. Suddenly she wondered what color it was, and pulled a strand in front of her face to look. Blond. What color had she imagined? She did not know. Suddenly, panic gripped her. She had no idea who she was, or where she was, or why she should be here. There seemed no world but this—a piece of ground, a tree, and a few small bushes. There was nothing else to be seen. She sank down beside the tree, put her head on her arms, and began to shiver.

Once again it was the demands of her body that forced her to action. After perhaps twenty minutes she lifted her head again and, still shaking, pulled herself upright by the tree. She might have spent forever clinging to the tree, but she pushed herself away from it, taking two wavering steps forward. At once the ground gave way before her feet and she found herself ankle-deep in water. She bent down, made a bowl of her two hands, and drank. A number of small, amphibious organisms went down with the water, but she did not notice them. She stood up with water dripping from her chin. There was still nothing to see, except—and now she noticed a rowboat half in, half out of the water just beside her. She saw that it was tied to the tree. It had no significance for her and she stepped back, a little stronger, a little more clearheaded, but still deeply anxious and frightened. Supporting herself on the tree, she turned her back on the water and pushed her way through the bushes. Even hindered by the mist it did not take her long to learn that she was on a very small island. The reason for the boat was explained. She returned and sat down beside it. There was no telling what lay beyond the island on any side. There seemed to be nothing at all, and in her bemused and bewildered mind came the thought that perhaps there was nothing at all. Perhaps this was all there was, and she was alone in an emptiness that had no purpose. There was no reason why she should do anything but simply sit here. So she sat motionless and again her head fell forward and, with her forehead on her knees, she slept once more.

It was her stomach that woke her the second time. A sudden cramp jolted her to wakefulness. This time it was not necessary to wonder where she was. There were the island, herself, and the little boat. She knew that. But now things had changed. The nothingness beyond the island was moving. It was changing shape as she watched it, and there were gradations in the quality of it. Now it was thick, dark, and slowly moving. Now it was pale and almost transparent. And at last through the swirling veils she saw a shining patch of water. Somewhere there was sunlight, and it was falling like hope itself on that one small piece of water. So there was water, and the nothing that had surrounded her was only mist. New life surged through her body. A kind of ecstasy took hold of her because she was not, after all, the only living thing, and it was water and not nothingness that surrounded the island. She laughed suddenly, and the laugh, just as suddenly, turned into a sob. But she had made a decision. She went back to the boat, untied the painter, and got in. She did not ask herself why it was she knew what to do, but pulled away from the island into the moving mist in search of food.

She rowed on, and quite soon she could no longer see the island. There was a moment when she wondered if there was anything but the island and the water, and if she lost the island she might row on forever, arriving nowhere. The moment passed. There was no food on the island. The mist moved round her, thickening, thinning, rising from the water and falling again, and now and then sunlight filtered through and showed her a still and mirrorlike surface. She made very little sound as she rowed, sliding the blades through the surface without a splash, lifting them out so that the drops of water ran off and fell only an inch or so, silently back into the dam.

Because she made so little sound she was able to hear the bird's cry when it came. For a moment she paused, resting on the oars. Then she turned the boat in the direction the sound had come from and began to row with purpose. It had been the high cry of a kestrel. She did not wonder how she knew, but she knew also that kestrels hunt on land and not on water. It was not only exertion that made her breath come faster. Yet when she suddenly burst through the mist and saw the bank of the dam so close, and the three people who stood there, she felt a sudden fear so powerful that she swung the boat again and rowed back into the mist and did not stop until even the voices had died away.

It was chance that brought her back to the island, for she was rowing blindly, still shaking with fear. For the second time she pulled the boat into the rushes and tied it to the tree. Then, for a second time she crawled under the bushes and lay panting while the trembling in her body subsided. As she lay there the mist cleared, the sun, low on the horizon, shone out over the water, and at last the whole of the dam and the hills, paddocks, homesteads, trees that surrounded it were clear to her. Before the last of the sunlight drained away she lifted her head, looked about, and sat up. She knew now that she was on an island in a large stretch of water, and that life was going on round its shores. But how she came to be there and why remained clouded in her mind. Sooner or later the need for food would drive her out, but she realized that there was no way she could make herself confront any other person and ask for help.

She sat, looking out across the dam while the sun set and the night came. Her thoughts became more rational now that a real world had appeared out of the mist. It was a world in which she belonged—somewhere. The problem of where she belonged might have worried her more if she had been less hungry. But now, after thirty-six hours without food, finding something to eat was all she could think of. She considered rowing to the shore again while it was dark, but the fear of losing her island was stronger for the time being than her hunger. If she again met someone on

the shore and she lost her island . . . She made up her mind
to go with the first light. She would hide the boat, walk to
the nearest house, and find herself some food while every-
body slept. She could take it back to the island and stay
safely there, hidden. People were enemies. Only the little
island and the water—especially the lovely, safe expanse of
water—were where she belonged. The night deepened and
the great upturned bowl of stars hung over her. But she
could not sleep. The protests from her outraged stomach
saw to that. By the time the dawn broke she was stiff with
cold and, once again, near despair. Now was the time she
had planned to go, but when, making a huge effort, she
tried to move, every bone in her body began to protest. For
the present she gave up, and as she lay there the day
brightened, the sun came up and warmed her, and after the
long night she slept.

She woke with the sun in her eyes and a number of small
insects trying to sit on her face. She brushed them away
and sat up. This time, warmed and relaxed, her body was
ready to obey. It took her some time to get to her feet and,
finally, into the boat. It was midmorning by the time she
pushed off, bent her back, and began to row for the nearest
shore. It happened to be the same shore she had reached
before. But everything looks different in a mist and it no
longer seemed the same. She had stopped to have another
long drink before she got into the boat, and she felt better
for it. But she was now acutely hungry and prepared to take
risks to find food. She rowed on, and the island grew small
in the distance. Once or twice she looked over her shoul-

der and each time saw that the shore was coming closer. But not once did she take the trouble to look directly behind.

When she knew she was almost upon the final shallows she rowed one strong, last stroke, shipped the oars, and turned with her hand out to ease the boat into the bank. It was then she saw the two figures just beside her on the grass. One was lying on its stomach, gazing at her with great curiosity. The other was standing, and now it spoke. "I'll help you." It stretched out its hand.

At once the same sudden panic fear engulfed her. The sound she started to make froze in her throat. Escape was the only thought in her mind, and at once she pushed off again, seized the oars, and frantically rowed away. She was facing them now and saw that both were standing. A boy and a girl, the boy full grown and therefore dangerous. As the distance between them widened and the first fear passed, she registered more clearly what she saw. Jeans and T-shirts, curious faces, not angry, and the boy with a quiet voice. But they were people and she must get away fast.

Her eyes never left them as she rowed. They were still standing watching her when she came to the island. She rowed on, and when the island was between her and the shore she turned the boat and pulled in. She hoped they would think she had gone on to the farther shore. Having moored the boat, she crept forward under the bushes and lay and watched them. She would not move again until she knew what they would do next. They seemed to stand there for an eternity, but eventually they walked away and disappeared among the trees. She still did not move, and presently the sound of a car engine came across the water, accelerated, struggled along in low gear, became fainter, and then faded altogether. Her body was wet with fear and it was a long time before her heart ceased its thumping and her breathing slowed. And it was longer still before she began to wonder what she had found to fear in two people who, she now realized, had only been trying to help her. But the fear was there, too strong for logic. For the first time she tried to probe into her memory. It told her nothing except that somewhere, just behind that blank wall, was a happening she had managed with too great success to forget.

For an hour or more she lay trying to muster courage to row to the shore again. There was no longer anyone where the two had been, but she looked for another landing place that might promise more seclusion—more safety. There were too many people now round about the farms that she could see, and sounds of the day's work came from every shore. But behind one long, thin promontory there seemed to be thick bush, and trees that came to the water's edge. If she could get to that without anyone noticing she might be able to tie up her boat unseen. She meant to go at once, having picked out her spot. But she was safe here. The island was her home and she had no wish at all to leave it. She lay trying to gather the will to set off again, and time passed. Perhaps she slept for a short period because the next time she looked up the sun had moved quite noticeably and was now leaning to the western horizon. It was afternoon and if she did not move soon the night would come again and she would be even hungrier. Already she had found that if she made any sudden movement her head began to swim. She crossed her arms on the ground in front of her and rested her chin on her hands. She looked carefully all over the dam for signs of activity, turning first one way and then another. The view was clear on all sides except the west, where it was obstructed by the many twists and turns, inlets, bays, and promontories that formed the western shore. But where she was able to see, all seemed clear. Nothing moved on the dam and the sounds from the shore appeared to have diminished. The tractors, or whatever they were, had stopped. All the sheep and cattle that she was able to see were either quietly cropping grass or lying down. She looked again to the west, for anything coming round that point would be very near before she was able to see it. But here, too, everything seemed quiet under the afternoon sun. That something might suddenly appear was a risk she realized she would have to take. If it was a boat with a motor she would hear it before it reached the point. If it had no motor, she might still escape in her rowboat. Even a sail would scarcely fill on such a still afternoon. In any case there was the water. She trusted the water. If worse came to the worst, it was the ultimate refuge. She worked her way back to the boat.

7

"Shall I take a turn?" said Emily.

For a moment hurt pride and relief battled together in Hubert's interior. Relief won and, not without difficulty, they exchanged places. "Can you row, Emily?" said Hubert as the boat ceased its violent rocking.

"Tell you in a minute," said Emily and picked up the oars.

The forward progress of the boat was not as the crow flew, but in a series of graceful curves as if it were describing some intricate maneuver on a graph. At last, however, it settled to a straight, or fairly straight, course.

Hubert had remained tactfully silent. Now he spoke. "Just a fraction to starboard, Emily."

"What the hell are you talking about?" Emily, red-faced and grim, absent-mindedly trailed one oar so that the boat swept in a semicircle.

"Not so far," said Hubert. He pointed. "That way."

She said nothing, but bent her head and took the oars

again in a ferocious grip. By degrees the boat took the course along Hubert's pointing finger and remained on it very creditably until they reached the point of a long promontory.

"Are you tired, Emily?" said Hubert when they reached the point.

"No," snapped Emily.

"Well, I'm glad because when we pass this point I want to be able to watch very carefully. We'll probably see the island and I don't want that girl dashing off again till we've had time to talk to her."

" 'Course, I can see it, too," said Emily. "But if that's how you want it. I'm not in the least tired." Her face had gone from pink to faintly purple, and her forehead shone wetly. But now Hubert was not thinking of Emily, but of what the view from round the point might show.

"But I'm very hungry," said Emily.

"So am I," said Hubert. "Go on, Emily. Row."

Emily's rowing was improving by the minute, and they swept smoothly round the point. The upper reaches of the dam lay open before them and there, quite near, was the island. The few stunted trees stood up like bristles, and low scrub totally clothed the small hump that was the island. In the indentations around its tiny shoreline were clumps of rushes. They could see no sign of life on it at all.

"We'll creep up on it very quietly," said Hubert.

"How?" said Emily. "I'm not splashing and you're the only one that's talking."

Hubert knew that hunger often made people irritable, so

now he only put his finger on his lips and said, "Shsh."
Emily looked at him with hatred.

They were very near the island when Hubert first saw
signs of movement on it. The bushes began to wave vio-
lently, something white, or whitish, detached itself from
them, and in a few minutes the bow of a rowboat appeared
from among the rushes.

"Quick, Emily! Row. Block her off."

No one ever called on Emily in vain, and now she bent
her back, reached forward, and plunged the oars into the
water. The boat sprang ahead and the waters parted like
the crossing of the Red Sea. Once more she reached forward, plunged the blades in, and pulled. The little boat
might have been a kangaroo.

"That'll do," said Hubert. "We've got her now." And
Emily slumped forward, panting.

The other boat was coming out stern first and the girl
in it was pushing frantically at the bank. Hubert leaned
over and took the boat as it was about to collide with their
own. Holding the gunwale firmly in both hands he said,
"It's all right. Honestly. There's no need to run. We only
want to help." The picture of that terrified face was still in
his mind's eye and when the girl turned to look at them
he saw it again, but this time to the terror was added
exhaustion and, it seemed, pain. There was nothing she
could do and she sank down, clutching the gunwale on
either side and staring at him. He thought she tried to say
something, but out of that tremulous and anguished
mouth the words would not come. "Honestly," said

Hubert again, "we can see you need help and we only want to help you."

Emily had shipped the oars and now sat watching. When the girl still said nothing she spoke. "You're hungry, aren't you?"

This time the girl nodded. Suddenly she said, "I'm terribly hungry," and burst into tears.

It was more than Hubert could stand. "You don't *have* to be hungry," he shouted. "We'll take you home. We'll give you all the food you want. I don't care why you're here, or what you've done—" He stopped suddenly and drew in his breath. He had not meant to say any of it. None of it was his business, anyway. It was the sight of that face that had got the better of him, that had undermined his better judgment. He looked at her now and wished he had not spoken.

Emily said, "My brother can't stand seeing anything or anyone in trouble. You're in trouble. You can't go on living on this tiny island. Sooner or later you'll have to come off. From the look of you I'd say it's time now." She stopped, thought for a minute, and then said, "I suppose we could bring you food. But you'd die of exposure, or something. Look, just tell us and, honestly, we'll help you. We're not the police or anything. We're perfectly harmless, aren't we, Hubert?"

Hubert had recovered himself. "Absolutely. And I'm Hubert and this is my sister, Emily. We saw you yesterday in the mist and that's why we came back today. No—we came for the specs, but when we saw you again we knew there was trouble somewhere. So tell us."

Some of the panic had drained from her face, but there was still a kind of desperation there, something that could not be accounted for. At last she spoke, and they noticed that she had a faint, unexpected accent. She looked up for the first time into their faces, unafraid. "You see, that's it. That's the trouble. I don't *know* why I'm here." It was almost a shriek and she began to cry again.

Emily looked at Hubert. Of all the answers they might have expected, this was the least likely. Hubert was looking at her, quite dazed. But Emily said briskly, "Then tell us how you got here." Bianca shook her head and suddenly plunged her face into her hands. Muffled through her fingers came words.

"I can't. I don't know." For a short time they all sat in silence. Then Hubert said, "This won't do. We've got to decide on something."

Again there was that look of near panic on the girl's face. Disregarding it, Emily said, "There's only one thing to do. We'll go home and let Dad sort it out. Hubert, you can row her boat and I'll bring this one back."

He had already begun to move when Bianca screamed, stood up, swayed for a moment in the rocking boat, put one foot on the gunwale, and plunged into the water. The last, safe, quiet refuge, the first mother, as Hubert would have said.

"Go after her, Hubert. Quick!" And for the second time in two days Emily pushed Hubert into the dam.

By the time he surfaced, Bianca was already swimming away from the island, out into the deep water, and her tangled hair streamed out over her back. He saw her at once and began to swim after her. Emily picked up the oars, clenched her teeth, and began to row. Bianca did not swim for long. She was too tired, too hungry, and too confused. To give up and let herself sink seemed the most peaceful thing she could do. She was going down when Hubert reached her and already she had stopped struggling. But when he took her arm and tried to turn her over on her back she resisted. She was still trying to break away from him when Emily brought the boat up beside them.

"Grab her other arm, Emily."

Somehow between them they got her half over the gunwale. Her head hung down and water gushed from her into the bottom of the boat. Her legs were still feebly trying to kick Hubert away, but her remaining strength had gone, and, leaning over, Emily took her legs in her arms, braced herself, and heaved. Bianca collapsed into the boat and ceased to move.

"Go on, Hubert. Get in. I think she might be dead."

Having got the girl out of the water, Hubert was taking his time about climbing in after her. Hearing Emily's words he appeared to levitate from the surface and propel himself over the side in one movement.

"Mouth to mouth. The kiss of life," said Emily. "Quick, Hubert."

Hubert had been gasping and coughing, but all at once he stopped. He looked at Emily with his mouth open and she thought he was going to be sick. "I can't," he said.

Emily scarcely stopped to think. "Well, tell me and I'll try. Help me turn her over." She put her knee on the thwart and tried to lift Bianca by the shoulders. Hubert moved at last to try to help her. But again, as soon as she felt the touch of a hand, Bianca began to struggle.

Hubert leaned back. "You see? She's not dead at all. Why did you say that, Emily?"

"I only thought she might be dead. So she isn't. So I think we've got to get her back to Dad as quick as we can. Don't you?"

"Yes." He was going to say something else but he stopped, and with an effort, said, "I'm sorry, Emily, about the mouth to mouth."

Emily was trying to get hold of Bianca's arm to move her off the rowing thwart, but now she looked at Hubert. It was not often she had the advantage of him. She saw the expression on his face, and looked away again and only said, "It wasn't necessary. Come on, Hubert. She's got to be moved whether she likes it or not."

By now Bianca's struggles were intermittent and feeble, and without too much difficulty they got her onto the stern thwart sitting up and leaning against Emily. Hubert took the oars and began to row. It was a long way back to the jetty and their mother's car. For some time Hubert rowed in silence and Bianca leaned against Emily with her eyes closed. Every so often her body was seized by a fit of shivering, and Emily clutched her fiercely in case she decided to go overboard again. After one of them Emily noticed that Bianca's eyes were open. Holding her tightly, Emily leaned over so that their heads were close together. She whispered, "What's your name?" and felt all the muscles tense.

Emily felt herself fixed by a wide, mindless stare. After

a long silence, while Hubert forgot to row, Bianca said in a voice that had lost all life and all expression, "That's the trouble. I can't remember." She seemed to have accepted that for the moment they meant her no harm, for she relaxed again and, after that long stare, her eyes closed. The fits of shivering became fewer. Hubert rowed on and after a time they rounded the point. The sun was low, but shading her eyes Emily could see the jetty. There was still a great deal of water between them and where the car was waiting. Bianca seemed to be sleeping, and Emily said, "Even if she doesn't want to come, we've got to take her back, haven't we? Something must have happened to make her lose her memory, mustn't it? Something awful?" Hubert was out of breath and only nodded. Emily went on, "It must have been pretty terrible if she'd rather drown."

When Hubert was able to speak again he said, "The funny thing is, I saw her face quite close before—before she went under. It was more as if she thought she had escaped. She looked quite—sort of—happy."

"She is bonkers," said Emily. "I thought so from the beginning."

If they thought Bianca was settling down and had accepted them at last as friends, they discovered their mistake as they came nearer to the jetty. Not long before they reached it she opened her eyes again. The first thing she saw was Hubert facing her, watching her, and at once she began to struggle. When she felt Emily's arms tighten round her she tried to break free.

"It's all right," said Emily. "Honestly, it's all right. Can't you see we're trying to help you? We're going to take you home. Our father's a doctor. He'll make you well again."

"I'm well. I'm well. I only want to get away. You don't know—" She stopped, and looked dazed.

"What don't we know?" said Hubert very quietly.

But she could not tell them. There had been a flash. For a moment it was as if a sudden shaft of light had broken through. But it went out again as quickly as it had come and she was left again, bewildered, frightened, and with only the overpowering determination to get away. The one thing she had learned was that these two appeared not to want to hurt her. But they did not know, and there was no way she could tell them that taking her among people was not the way to keep her safe. She saw the jetty coming nearer with every stroke of Hubert's oars, she saw the sheds and buildings behind it, and in spite of her painful hunger she began to plan a way of escape. It seemed again as if the waters of the dam were her only sanctuary.

Emily began to chatter. "We'll take you home, feed you up, get you warm again, and I wouldn't be surprised if that makes everything right. I think you're just too cold, too hungry, and too frightened—of something." She waited, but Bianca said nothing. "If it doesn't, Dad'll be able to fix you up."

She could not see Bianca's face as she spoke, but Hubert could, and he said, "You'd better stop, Emily. You're not really doing any good. I think you might be making it all more difficult." He rowed on, and the jetty came closer with every stroke, and Bianca watched it as if she were hypnotized. Emily felt the tension growing in her and braced herself for any sudden action. It was Hubert who broke the silence.

"Can you tell us what you'd like us to do with you? You need food and shelter, don't you? And you didn't find those on that little island. So what shall we do?"

"I don't know. I don't know." She began to cry.

He lifted the oars and let the boat drift. He turned his head and looked along the shore, and Emily, watching, saw the exact moment when the solution came to him. After a moment he said, "Emily, what are we thinking of? There's the trailer."

"Of course. Hubert, you are clever." She beamed at him.

"Can you find it, Emily? You were there last—when you and Mum cleaned it out."

"That was a month ago," said Emily. "I remember how to get there. But—Hubert—it's tucked away in the scrub. Can we really leave her there?"

"You think of something better. I can't see us forcing her into the car. We left it near the man's boat shed, remember? And I can't see us driving all the way home with her probably screaming and trying to jump out." He was talking as if Bianca were deaf, or an imbecile, but there seemed no other way. That she was neither was clear from the way her eyes were fixed on him.

"Ask her," said Emily. "You ask her then, Hubert. I only seem to frighten her."

So Hubert leaned forward over the oars and said with his face very near Bianca's, "Our father's fishing trailer is in among some trees quite far from anywhere else. Would you like it if we hid you there tonight and we'll come in the morning when you've decided what you want to do."

"How do you plan to come?" said Emily. "Tomorrow's Monday and it's Mum's car."

"Shut up, Emily," said Hubert.

They both saw her lift her head and look about her. The island was out of sight, but the waters of the dam lay all round them, stretching into the distance. It was very still, shining in the late, level sunshine. Perhaps she found it inviting, as she had seemed to find it earlier. But as they waited for her to answer, a small evening breeze sprang up and the mirror surface shattered and grew dark, hiding what was below and wiping out in one silent moment all that it had revealed of what was above.

"There'll be blankets," said Emily. "And the food will be hot."

She spoke at last, but what she said surprised them both. She leaned toward Hubert, peered into his face, and said, "What am I going to do?"

Hubert smiled. A warming, friendly smile. It was a response Emily would never have thought of making, and when he said, "That's what you're going to do," she nodded her head and sank back into Emily's arms. But they all knew that had not been what she had meant. Hubert slid the blades back into the water. "Where, Emily?" he said.

She pointed to a thick grove of trees that came down to the water's edge some distance from the jetty. Behind it the wilderness of the Nature Reserve stretched unbroken for some distance. Hubert turned the boat and made for it. As he rowed he smiled again at Bianca and said, "If you haven't decided anything by the morning we'll work it out for you. You'll see. It'll be all right."

Hubert headed the boat now at an angle, away from the boat shed and, watching their direction, Emily said, "Go on past the trees a bit, Hubert. We don't want the man at the boat shed seeing where we go ashore."

They pulled in discreetly among the roots of a big tree. Emily let Bianca go for the first time and jumped ashore. Hubert handed her the painter and took hold of the roots. Not once did he let Bianca out of his sight. But there was no longer any need for caution. It was difficult even to get Bianca out of the boat. She could scarcely stand, and balancing while she stepped out of the boat and onto the bank was beyond her. In the end Hubert went, knee-deep, into the dam and lifted her out. While Emily held her he secured the boat and stepped ashore. Between them they half carried Bianca away from the water and into the trees. The trailer was not far away, carefully hidden in a grove of saplings.

Hubert unlocked the door and went in. Emily pushed Bianca in after him and sat her by the table while Hubert let down the bed and got out the bedding. Between them they spread out the blankets and found a pillow. "No sheets or pillowslips," said Hubert, "but you can't have everything. You'll do very well here for the night, I think." He spoke cheerfully, as if plucking girls off islands and keeping them hidden were something he did every day of the week.

Perhaps his light-hearted manner was what Bianca needed, for now she stood up, supporting herself on the table, and said, "You're so kind. I—it's dreadful to be alone."

"You're not alone anymore," said Emily. "Everything's going to work out, you'll see. Here. Let me get those wet clothes off you. Go out, Hubert, while I get her under the blankets."

Bianca now seemed totally acquiescent and there was no trouble in getting her into bed, or in getting her to promise not to move for any reason ("Except," said practical Emily, "for going outside to pee, of course.") until they came again. She only asked that they should shut the door and close up the trailer when they went. By the time they left her she was already getting warmer and was half asleep. They closed the door softly and went down to the boat.

"Now," said Emily. "We'd better hurry, or he'll be charging overtime, or something, for the boat."

"It seems to me," said Hubert as they rowed away, "that we're scarcely halfway there. One or two problems loom ahead."

"It was you who wouldn't take her home. That's what I wanted to do from the beginning."

"It just didn't seem possible," said Hubert.

"You mean you were too soft. I would have been *firm.*"

"I know, Emily. Everyone says you're the *firm* one."

"No need to be nasty. Go on, Hubert. Hurry. It's nearly dark."

The boatman was standing on the jetty waiting for them.

He took the painter from Emily and pulled them alongside. "Only just made it," he said. "I'd have had to charge you overtime. Besides me own time going to look for you."

"Would you have?" said Emily. She really wanted to know. "Would you have gone looking for us?"

"Looking for me boat more like." The boatman was a no-nonsense man. "Come on. Hop out so I can put it away."

"Good night," they both said as they walked over to their car. They did not hear if he replied. They rather thought he had not bothered. Emily produced the car key from her pocket, slightly to Hubert's surprise, and they got in. By the time the car moved off, its lights making a golden road of the dirt track, the dam was already dark. The only other light came from the boatman's window, and far out on the water the other rowboat, its painter trailing, floated off over the black water, taken very slowly away from the island by the breeze.

8

Hubert and Emily were silent for most of the drive home. As they came into the town Hubert said, "How are we going to take the car out later, Emily, without it looking funny?"

As Emily had been asking herself the same question for most of the journey, she was now able to say with some confidence, "Leave it to me, Hubert."

They were met at the door by Paul, runny-nosed and furious. "You went to the dam again without me."

Emily pushed him aside and went straight to the kitchen. Her mother was, as usual at this time of day, bent over the stove. "We're back, Mum. Sorry we're a bit late. We thought we'd go for a row."

Mrs. Hamilton whirled round. "A bit late! We were thinking of getting the police."

"Mum, you know you weren't. We're not late for dinner, even."

Mrs. Hamilton attacked on another front. "Anyway, where are the glasses?"

"Here, Mum. We found them." Emily began fishing in her pockets. When her fingers came in contact with the glasses she ignored them and went on fishing. At last, looking at her mother with a face of horror, she said, "We must have left them. We must have left them behind after all." Hubert was standing behind her, and now she turned on him. "Hubert, remember when I put them on that rock and said, 'I'll put them in my pocket soon as I've blown my nose'?" Hubert nodded, full of admiration for his sister. Perhaps he nodded with a little too much enthusiasm, for he noticed that Mrs. Hamilton was now looking at him. Perhaps it was only guilt that made him think there was suspicion in her look. At any rate, something made him say, "Emily, I think we should go back and get them *at once!*"

"Whatever made you blow your nose?" said Mrs. Hamilton tragically.

"One has to sometimes. You know. Look, Mum, could we have dinner first, frightfully quickly, and then go back for them? I don't think they should be left overnight, do you? Anything might happen."

Mrs. Hamilton had visions of kangaroos knocking them off the rock, or even pocketing them, of eagles, fascinated by the glint of glass in the dawn, bearing them off to some distant aerie. If her nature study was a little vague, the pictures were very vivid. "Oh dear," she said. "Very well."

After dinner there was a hurried and furtive hunt for food, unproductive as they had just eaten it all and considerably hampered by Paul, who had now determined not to let them out of his sight. In the end Hubert managed to hiss at Emily, "I've got some more money out of the housekeeping tin. We'll have to buy the food. Come on."

Paul barred the way. "I'm coming with you," he shrieked.

To their relief Mrs. Hamilton now bore down on him. "Oh no you're not. You shouldn't even be out of bed with your cold." And she swept him off, and his frustrated bellows died away as they ran for the car.

"Emily," said Hubert when they were well out of earshot, "you were terrific."

"It worked, anyway," said Emily. "And telling lies isn't as bad as stealing the housekeeping money. How'll we ever pay it back?"

"I don't really think we can. But, see, Emily, the way I'm coming to look at it, pretty soon we'll just have to tell them about the girl, and that'll explain how we came to take the money. They'd never expect us to let her starve to death."

"They might expect us to bring her straight home."

"Yes—well—" Hubert sighed. "All we can say is we did what we thought best."

"I know just what Dad'll say. 'It wasn't up to you to decide what was best.' "

Hubert sighed again. "Sometimes I find you quite depressing, Emily."

"We've just got to face it." Emily's tone was infuriatingly bracing. "Where shall we buy the food? There's not much open at this time of night—not much hot."

In the end they managed to get some hot meat pies,

spring chicken rolls, and a hamburger. "Fruit," said Emily. "It'll counteract all that fat." So they bought two apples, two bananas, and an orange.

"That'll probably kill her," said Hubert, "on her empty stomach."

"Oh well," said Emily. "It's the best we can do. Let's hurry."

"What about the glasses?"

"I left them on the sideboard."

"Emily! You didn't! What if Mum finds them?"

"She won't. They're under the hot plate."

"Good God," said Hubert, and put his foot down hard on the accelerator.

This time, and after some argument, they turned off the road that led to the dam wall before they came to the boathouse, and wound their way along a rough and twisting track that led at last to the water's edge. "Can we turn?" asked Emily as they got out.

"I'm certainly not backing all that way to the road," said Hubert. "And other people must have turned."

"Oh well," said Emily. "Come on, then. This way."

Hubert followed, laden with most of the food, though Emily carried the fruit "so it won't get bruised." He had complete confidence in her ability to find the way. Emily seldom got lost. She pushed her way now through the low scrub, following the ghost of a track he could not even see. Once she stopped, and all of a sudden the bush fell very quiet. The small breeze still agitated the tops of the trees with a secret, whispering noise. Otherwise there was no other sound. Even the night birds were silent. After a moment she moved on again and Hubert followed as nearly as possible in her footsteps. At last, when the hot food was growing cold and had become curiously heavy, a dim whiteness loomed up in front of them and Emily said, "Here we are." She stepped out into the clearing and went up to the trailer door.

"Just a minute," said Hubert.

"What's the matter?"

"I don't think we should just burst in."

"I wasn't going to burst in exactly. I was just going to open the door." Her voice was huffy.

"Well, let me." He pushed her as tactfully as he could out of the way and stood close up against the door. He knocked very softly and said, equally softly, "It's us. We're here. With the food." For a long time they waited. But the door did not open and no sound came from inside. Hubert knocked again, louder. There was still no sound and no-body opened the door.

"She's dead," said Emily.

But Hubert was opening the door. Even now he did not go in, but put his head in and said again, "It's us. With the food." He was answered by a sort of sigh, and when Emily at last stepped in behind him she thought she could see a small mound pressed against one corner of the wall and the end of the bed. A sort of moan came from it. "I didn't know. I thought—" They never knew what she thought because her voice trailed away.

"We told you we'd come back," said Hubert. "But we thought you might be asleep. You were nearly asleep when we left."

The trailer was almost totally dark, and there were fumbling noises as Hubert felt in the drawers of the cupboard. Finally he grunted and shortly afterward a match flared as he put it to the candle he had found. "Thought I remembered where Dad had left them," he said with satisfaction. He poked it into the one candlestick and put it on the table. They could see her now—a small bundle still pressed against the wall with a grayish blue face and enormous eyes.

"You don't have to be frightened anymore," said Emily. "You can see it's only us. And get under the blankets for goodness sake. I can see you shivering."

Bianca slid down and pulled the blankets up to her chin. Her eyes were now on Hubert. "I did sleep," she said at last. "But these awful tummyaches woke me up."

"That's hunger," said Emily. "Come on. Eat these things we've brought. It's not much but it was the best we could do so late at night." Bianca almost snatched the meat pie that Emily held out, and crammed it into her mouth. "You'd better eat it slowly, or you might get a worse pain. You're not supposed to eat a lot all at once when you've been starving. I suppose you've been starving?"

"Yes," said Bianca and continued to demolish the pie. Hubert came and sat on the edge of the bed.

Emily said, "If there's still water in the tank and if the gas cylinder still works I'm going to make you some coffee—if there's any coffee."

There was silence then for some time, while Emily dealt with the stove and the water and the coffee and while Bianca continued to eat. Hubert sat and watched her. He began to frown, and after a time he said, "I do think you ought to stop for a while. Don't you, Emily?"

"Yes, but I expect it's hard to if you've been starving," said Emily without looking round. She had just got the stove to go.

When Bianca had finished the spring roll she had been eating she did stop, and she looked up at Hubert, sitting beside her, and for the first time she smiled. The transformation was astonishing. Hubert, who had been watching her face anxiously as the spring roll disappeared, opened his eyes very wide and forgot to take the next breath. It was not only what the smile had done to that tired face, it was that for the first time he found himself looking at a real person. Up to now she had been no more to him than something rather badly needing help—something he undoubtedly felt sorry for, as he would have felt sorry for any starving and terrified creature. But here was a real girl, who was not simply terrified and starving, but who now began to react to him and Emily in a perfectly human way. He forgot for the moment that she lived only in the present, and said, "What's your name?"

Her smile faded. After what seemed a very long time she said, "I can't remember."

"It doesn't matter," said Emily, who came to the bed now, carrying a mug. "Don't worry about it. You'll remember soon. Look, here's your coffee. No milk, I'm afraid, but have it while it's hot." And she put the mug carefully into Bianca's two hands. They watched while she drank it and, little by little, saw the gray-white look leave her face. When she had finished it she handed the mug back to Emily and said for the second time, "What shall I do?" And now it was a question that had been puzzling them, too.

Hubert leaned forward and his hand fell on her knee. It was warm beneath the blanket. "There's no need to worry. I'm sure Emily's right and you'll remember soon. But is there anything—anything at all—that you could tell us that might give us some idea of where you belong? You see, it could be just a matter of getting you home again."

It was clear she was trying to remember. She looked straight at Hubert without seeing him, and she began to frown. Then her face suddenly crumpled and she covered it with her hands.

"I'm sure you needn't cry," said Emily. "We're going to look after you, you know."

They waited while she recovered. When she took her hands from her face again Emily handed her a tissue and said, "I think we've got to—"

Hubert shook his head quickly. When he was sure she was not going to continue he said, "We'll just sit here while you digest that stuff. There's plenty of time."

"But Mum'll be—" This time Emily stopped because Hubert had kicked her shin.

"There'll be no problem. Sit down, Emily. I'm going to tell—I say, we'll have to call you something. What shall we call you?"

Bianca opened her mouth to speak, shut it again and then, in a strange kind of whisper, said, "Call me Bianca."

"That's an odd name," said Emily. "Never mind. It'll do till you remember your own. Go on, Hubert."

"Right. I'm going to tell Bianca—it is an odd name, isn't

it?—who we are and what we do. Just so she knows who she's dealing with. I'm Hubert Hamilton and this is Emily." He continued to speak quietly and slowly, describing their home and their activities, telling her how he aimed to be a doctor like his father, how Emily still had a few more years to go at school, how Paul was a much younger and frequently troublesome brother.

"Oh, Hubert, he's not," said Emily. "He's no worse than any other little boy of five. I think he's rather nice, really."

"Matter of opinion," said Hubert. "He's probably par for the course and he's bound to improve. He won't be forever falling into dams and losing his glasses." Bianca was watching him carefully and he noticed with some satisfaction that the tension was leaving her and once again she had begun to smile. He pressed on, telling her about his parents and the dog they once had, and the cat they had now. The cat, he said, had just had kittens.

She looked up quickly and said, "Did she eat them?"

"Eat them?" said Emily. "Of course not. They were *her* kittens."

"Cats sometimes eat their kittens," said Bianca. "Our cat did."

There was a sudden silence. Hubert and Emily sat very still. The candle, burning low, flickered a little, sending shadows leaping about the trailer roof. Outside, the wind had begun to rise and the trees moaned gently over them. Bianca had stopped talking and had given up looking at Hubert, and seemed to be gazing at the dancing shadows. Her mouth was still half open. Presently, very softly, Hubert said, "Tell us."

She shivered and her eyes focused again. She breathed in deeply. Then she spoke. "It was horrid—beastly. We had this little cat. She came in out of the bush and she was only young, but she was going to have kittens. So we put some bags down for her in the shed. I went into the shed one morning—and there she was. On the bags. And I could see her eyes shining as she looked at me. And she had one kitten in her mouth and she was *eating* it." The last words were a shriek of horror and she clapped her hands over her face and began to shake. Behind the hands they could hear little moaning noises. Emily and Hubert held her between them until she stopped shaking. She let her hands drop and looked into Hubert's face and said, "You see, she was their *mother*. They would have expected her to protect them. And instead she *ate* them." Her head, wrapped in her arms, fell forward on her knees. There was no consoling her now, and Hubert and Emily could only sit and wait. Over her head they looked at one another blankly, at a loss both for words and for what decision to make next. It seemed a long time before she began to quiet down.

When she had been silent for some time Emily said, "What shall we do, Hubert?"

But Hubert for once was baffled and dismayed. No such situation had ever presented itself to him before. Emotions of these proportions made him feel numb inside. His brain felt numb too. He could only shake his head and feel helpless.

So it was now Emily who said, in a tone that was not at

all her usual one, "She'll just have to come home with us. We can't leave her here. You tell her, Hubert."

Hubert leaned forward, took hold of her shoulders, and gently lifted her head off her knees. Her face was once again the desperate, panicked face that they had pulled out of the water. Her eyes darted from one corner of the trailer to the other. "I have to get away. I have to get away," was all she seemed able to say, and she began to struggle as Hubert held her.

This time Emily stood up and came over to the bed and helped Hubert hold her. "You're not well, Bianca," she said in her most practical voice. "You heard Hubert say our father's a doctor. We're going to take you to him now—tonight." And she began to peel back the blankets.

Bianca now began to fight in earnest. She struggled, she kicked, she tried to bite, and there was nothing in her face but mindless panic. And at last she broke away from them and would have rushed to the door if Hubert had not got there first. She tried to claw her way to the window, but it was not made to open and she sank down under it. "It's hopeless, Emily," said Hubert with his back to the door. "We're undoing everything we've managed to do."

"Right," said Emily, suddenly masterful. She went to Bianca, took her by the shoulders and shook her. Then she lifted her onto the bed again and slapped her face. "I know you should do this," she told Hubert over her shoulder. "We were told."

Bianca subsided and Emily pushed her down onto the bed and pulled the blankets over her. Then she spoke. "So we won't take you with us, Bianca. But we have to go. You're to stay here quietly—alone—and there'll be more food tomorrow. We'll leave you alone, but we'll be back. We're not going to take you anywhere. You can trust us—honestly. So just stay quiet."

The candle suddenly glimmered once and went out and the trailer was dark. The smell of burning wax floated on the disturbed air. Emily felt her way to Hubert and when she touched him, said, "Come on. We've got to go." Hubert followed her out and shut the trailer door behind him. They said nothing as they tramped their way back to the car. The situation had resolved itself and there was nothing left to say. They spoke only once as they drove home.

As he swung the car off the dirt track and onto the paved road, Hubert said, "You noticed, didn't you, Emily, that she's beginning to remember things?"

"That cat business. Wasn't it horrible? Do you think we should have asked her more then, while she was remembering?"

Hubert sighed despairingly. "I don't know. I had a feeling we could wreck it by pressing her too hard. Besides, I didn't want to interrupt. I thought we might hear more."

"I expect you're right." After a pause she said, "You do see now, we've got to tell Dad. It's too much for us to deal with. Isn't it, Hubert?" When he did not answer at once she said again, "Isn't it, Hubert?"

He glanced round at her then and his face was troubled. "She just doesn't want people. That's all it is. It was lucky she came to accept us. To bring anyone else to the trailer is a sort of betrayal, isn't it, Emily?"

"Well, you tell me what else we can do."

But he could not, and at last they drove in at their own gate and into the garage. All the lights in the house were on, and their mother was standing at the door. She was not given to nagging, or making unnecessary complaints, and she did not now. But they could see her face under the porch light, and Emily ran and put her arms round her, and led her inside before any word was spoken.

9

Having spoken to his friends at the police station, Doctor Hamilton had been anxious to see Frances when he began his rounds at the hospital the next morning. He understood she had agreed to remain in the hospital overnight on condition that a search was begun immediately for her daughter. She was assured that it would start as soon as she had left the station and that when anything was known, or—here the sergeant coughed apologetically—discovered, she would be told. There was nothing she could do, they told her, except keep out of their way and recover.

So Dr. Hamilton was not pleased when the matron of the hospital met him when he arrived with the news that Frances had discharged herself almost at first light, and had gone off, they did not know where.

"Was she asked?"

"Of course, Doctor. She said she hadn't made up her mind."

"Couldn't you have stopped her? She'd had a pretty

hefty sedative. She must at least have been vague. I'd have thought she'd still have been drowsy."

"She was. But she was quite determined and we had no authority to stop her if she wanted to go."

"Why didn't you telephone me?"

The matron gave a small cough. "It was very early, and it didn't seem, you understand, to be a crisis situation. There was nothing really wrong with her."

"She lives quite a long way from here. She would have had no money and no car."

In the most tactful way she knew, the matron explained that it was not the hospital's job to keep tally of information of this kind. "As a matter of fact, I had intended to put the social worker onto her as soon as she turns up. She should be here at any moment." The matron looked around as if the social worker might have materialized through the vinyl tiles behind her.

Doctor Hamilton looked at the vinyl tiles too, but he was not expecting to find the social worker, and his mind was busy. Matron waited, confident that her hospital's reputation was safe in her hands. At last he looked up. "Look, Matron, ring the police station, will you, and just tell them. I'll try to see them myself as soon as I've finished here."

In the end there were too many pressing incidents during the day—what the matron would have referred to as "crisis situations"—for him to find the time. He knew the police would have been informed, so he was not greatly worried, but the thought of Frances was never very far from the surface of his mind, and as he went about the town he found himself looking for a sight of her. When he saw one of the half dozen town taxis pulled up at the taxi rank, he stopped behind it and got out.

"Hi, Doc," said the driver, putting down the racing tips. "What can I do for you?"

"Just wondered if you'd seen a young—youngish—woman about town this morning. She should still be in the hospital but she walked out. I don't think she'd have been thinking of hiring you. To my knowledge she had no money with her. It's a longish story, but I'd rather like to know what's become of her. I thought you might have seen her sort of wandering about. She could have been a bit vague."

"Funny you should ask that." The driver seemed a little vague himself, and went into a kind of trance. It was clear that something would emerge in due time, and Doctor Hamilton waited. At last he scratched his head and said, "Trying to remember, see? There was a woman. Now where was it? Corner of Peel and Thorn Streets. I seen her when I was coming along to the rank. She was talking to Bob—you know, drives the Falcon taxi. What did you say her age would be?"

"I didn't say, actually, but she'd be about thirty-seven. Fair, was she?"

The driver was now looking into the far distance and after a moment said, "Reckon she was. Kind of blond. They seemed to be having quite a natter."

"Did she get into the taxi, did you notice?"

"Did she now?" He suddenly took his eyes from the

distant prospect and fixed them on Doctor Hamilton's face. "Yes. She did, Doc. She got in and Bob drove off. Come to think of it, that was early and I haven't seen 'im since."

"I see. Well, thanks, Arthur. That's very helpful." Doctor Hamilton drove off and Arthur returned to his racing tips.

So she had gone home. When he got back to his office later in the day he phoned the police station. There was no further news, but they were glad to know where she was—or might be. The girl had not turned up yet, but there was no reason to think she would not turn up somewhere.

"She'd have to, see?" said the sergeant. "She'd need food and so on, and there's no reason to think there's been foul play. We're not too worried."

"No," said Doctor Hamilton. "I suppose not." But he found himself worrying just the same.

Frances could have simply got into the taxi and let him drive off, not telling him until she had reached home that she did not have enough money to pay the fare. He might then have taken a check, or she might have given him one of her possessions, like a watch, but even in her extremity she could not make herself do it. The price she paid was higher, though it failed to benefit the taxi driver. She told him the whole detailed, frightening story from the beginning. And because she was clearly desperate and because he had daughters of his own, he let himself be persuaded. "Hop in, lady," he said, "and tell me where you want to go."

She sat beside him and told him the way, and when they came to the small town where Bianca went to school and where Frances did her shopping she made him stop while she went into the store. She was gone some time and when she came out again the driver knew she had found out nothing. He thought she might be going to faint, and he opened the taxi door quickly.

"Here. Sit down."

She sat down and looked at him. "I'd better go home."

Then he said, "You told me they cut your telephone?" She nodded. "You'd better report it, hadn't you, while you're here? Don't suppose you thought of doing that— before?"

"No. Of course. Oh, thank you."

She got out, but before she walked off he said, "What about food? You got enough at home? Bread?"

She went back to the store and reappeared shortly afterward with her arms full. He got out and helped her put the groceries in the taxi. "It wasn't fixed," she said. "The girl on the exchange said she'd thought it must be out. She's reporting it, and said she'd tell the linesmen to hurry because it's an emergency." For a moment Frances's voice wavered. "They're kind, aren't they? You're kind, too. I don't know what I'd do—"

"Come on. Get in. I'll take you home." The driver sounded almost cross and he drove off in a great hurry.

She was leaning forward on the seat, clutching the edge of the instrument panel as they drove up to the garden gate. The house appeared to be as she had left it. The door was shut. She looked quickly at the chimney, but there was no smoke. In the yard the cow stood waiting for its daily bundle of hay. Beside it the calf was lying sleeping, full of unaccustomed milk. There was still no sign of the dog. The driver stopped the taxi and said, "I'll come in with you—help carry the parcels."

She had already flung open the car door and was making for the gate. She had forgotten the groceries, and the driver collected them and followed. She almost ran to the back door.

She stopped when she reached it and turned. "I—I forgot. I don't believe I locked it." She might have been apologizing to the taxi driver. She put her hand on the door handle and turned it. The door opened at once and she disappeared inside. Behind her the taxi driver stepped in, went over to the kitchen table, and dropped the groceries. She was already through the kitchen and into the hall beyond. He heard her calling, "Bianca! Bianca!" Then she came back, and he saw her hands trembling as she let herself carefully down onto the chair. She looked up at him. "She's not here," she said, and again he thought she was going to faint.

"Here," he said. "I'll get you a cuppertea. Where's your jug?" She hardly seemed to notice as he bustled about, finding things. She seemed surprised when a cup appeared under her nose. He was peering into the refrigerator, and now he returned to the table with a jug of milk held to his nose. "Seems OK," he said. "Don't know if you take milk? There you are, then. Go on. Drink it. Do you good."

At last she seemed to register and she looked up and tried to smile. "You're very kind," she said. "What about you? Will you have a cup?"

"Why not?" he said, and went to the cupboard and fetched himself a mug. She watched as he poured his own tea, helped himself to the milk, and then went to find the sugar. When he began to drink she picked up her own cup. At last he got up. "Better be getting on," he said, and looked doubtful. "You going to be all right?"

"Yes. Yes, I'm sure I shall. And I have to be here. You see that, don't you? I can't not be at home if—if—"

He went to the door. "I hope they fix your phone."

Suddenly she stood up too. "Stop. I nearly forgot. Just a minute. There's some money in the house somewhere. It mightn't be enough, but—you'd better take what there is. And leave me your address."

In the end he left his address and went, saying she might need the cash she had. She heard him drive off. A nice man. A friend. She suddenly put her hand over her mouth. It was very quiet after he had gone. A mist, creeping up from the dam, had enfolded the house and the yards and all the sheds. She sat for a long time looking down into her empty cup. After a still longer time she got up and went outside. She threw hay to the cow and let out the hens. They rushed past her, clucking indignantly. Automatically she collected the eggs. Spring had come to the fowl yard as well as to everywhere else and she counted fourteen eggs.

All about her life went on as usual. Not quite as usual. She went automatically to let the dog off the chain but the kennel was empty. The broken chain lay on the ground. She began to walk about the sheds and yard looking for the dog. He had never failed to come home before. But there was no sign of him. She stopped and listened. She could not have said what she expected to hear. But there was no sound at all. Soon, as the mist precipitated on the roof and the leaves, there would be small sounds as the drops ran off and fell onto the ground, but this had not yet begun. Going back into the house seemed like giving up hope, but she could not stand forever while the mist tangled in her hair and on the wool of her jacket. After a long time she went in again and shut the door behind her. She did not sit down, but went into Bianca's room and looked at the untidy bed where she herself had lain, the pile of books beside it, the collections of strange objects on shelves that Bianca had collected from time to time as her interests swung from one thing to another—small pebbles, gumnuts, cicada shells, pieces of bark, birds' eggs, photographs of landscapes and water and one of herself, a very small calculator. The biography of Bianca's life lay before her and, finding it unbearable, she went out again quickly, banging the door behind her.

It was not until the next morning that the police came. She could not have said how the night had passed, but she was sitting at the table in the kitchen again when they knocked on the door. She was up and opening it before the constable had had time to step back. The face that she presented to him was radiant with hope—and he saw the light fade from it as she saw only two men in blue standing before her.

"I thought—" she said.

"We'd like to ask you a couple of questions, Mrs. Bellini. May we come in?"

She had stepped back into the kitchen before she noticed the constable's hesitation. She saw now that the other policeman was holding her dog on a chain. "Where did you find him?" she said. "I lost him."

Instead of answering he said, "We saw he was yours by the disk on his collar. Can we tie him somewhere?"

"The kennel. Over there." She pointed across the yard. He followed her in while the dog was led off. As she sat down again she said, "Where did you find him? He's never been lost before."

"That's what we want to talk to you about." He would have continued, but she interrupted.

"I thought—you'd come to say you'd found Bianca."

The constable cleared his throat. "We've got a lot of chaps out, Mrs. Bellini. It's only a matter of time." He stopped and looked at the door. He seemed to be needing his companion's moral support.

"I see." Frances was studying the hands in her lap. "What were the questions?"

Before he could answer the other constable returned, rubbing his hands on the legs of his trousers. "Seemed quite pleased to be tied up," he said, as if this, at least, would be welcome news. "Looks a bit hollow, though. Got any dog biscuits?"

Frances jumped to her feet. "Oh. Yes. He hasn't been

fed." She would have gone at once, but the first constable put his hand on her arm as she brushed past. "He'll be OK for a few minutes, Mrs. Bellini. We'd just like a little talk first."

It was a mild enough statement, but it seemed to hit her like a blow. "You don't—you haven't—?" She sat quickly on the chair again and took hold of the edge of the table. "Tell me."

"Mrs. Bellini, we haven't so far found anything. We just wanted to know—was your daughter in the habit of rowing on the dam? Could she have crossed it, do you think, and perhaps gone away somewhere on the other side?"

"No," said Frances at once. "How could she? We haven't got a boat anymore. Besides—" They never found out what that was, for she suddenly drew in her breath and then said, "I'd forgotten. Our neighbors have a boat, and once or twice I believe they've taken her fishing. Not often. Not recently. Why?"

"Because this morning we found a rowboat washed up against the bank not too far from your boundary. We thought it might be yours." He did not tell her that the oars had been trailing, unshipped, as if the occupant had left the boat suddenly and unexpectedly. He was doing his duty, but, like the taxi driver, he was a kindly man. He stopped and saw that she was looking at him blankly. Unwillingly he continued. "We're asking because that's where we found your dog—on the bank by the boat."

After a long pause she said, "What do you mean? What are you thinking?" He saw the suspicion dawn on her face. In a whisper she said, "It's not true."

"That's all we know," he said quickly. "That's why we thought it was possible she may have cast the boat off when she left it—if she took it. So we're looking all round the lake now, Mrs. Bellini—farther afield than we thought necessary at first." Suddenly he put his hand over hers, perhaps because it was tearing holes in the cuff of her sweater. "We'll find her. Just a matter of time. But now we'd like you to tell us how we can reach the neighbor who owns the boat. We'd like to have a word with him." He got up. "We'll keep in touch with you and if you don't hear anything that'll be because there's nothing to tell." The two men went to the door. The constable who had been speaking stopped and seemed to look about the kitchen. "You got anyone here with you?" She shook her head. "Look, why don't I ask the neighbors if they could send someone to be with you, just for a short time?"

Now she got up. "No. No, thank you. I'd rather—just—wait."

She thought they had gone, but the other constable put his head round the door. "Don't forget to feed the dog." He smiled and was gone.

It was that last remark that brought her back to reality, that put her feet on the ground again. When they had gone she went out, fed and patted the dog, shut up the calf, and fed the fowls. Then she went back to the house to wait.

10

In Doctor Hamilton's house the lights went on burning long after all the other lights of the town were out. He was waiting for them when Emily and Hubert came with their mother into the house. "Come into my office," was all he said.

Mrs. Hamilton said rather quickly, "I think I'll—we'll all have coffee," and she slid out of Emily's grip and would have sped off, but Hubert said, "Mum, look, we've got something to say. We'd like you both to hear it. Wouldn't we, Emily?"

"It's important," said Emily.

Mrs. Hamilton looked at her husband. It was an enquiring look, and he said, "If it's going to be some kind of an excuse—I expect you've got one—it won't be necessary to keep your mother out of her bed any longer."

"But it isn't. Honestly. We want to tell you *both*. Don't we, Hubert?" The tone of righteous indignation is usually convincing, and when Hubert added, "It's important.

Really," Doctor Hamilton said, "Very well, then. Come on, Mary," and led the way into his office.

"See, there's this girl," said Emily as they sat down. "We thought at first she'd gone bananas—you know, mad—"

"Better let me tell it, Emily."

"I think so," said their father. "Much better. Go on, Hubert."

Emily's protest died at once when she saw their father's sudden alert look of interest. She folded her hands and gazed with admirable self-control at Hubert as he described their first sight of Bianca, of their return to look for her, and of her subsequent rescue by Hubert. When Mrs. Hamilton made a small murmur of approval Hubert said quickly, "It wasn't so great. Like when Paul fell in, Emily pushed me in both times." He saw his father smile, but the look of warm affection on Mrs. Hamilton's face was reward enough for honesty.

"He would have gone anyway," said Emily. "He's just slower than me. That's all."

"It's true," said Hubert. "But, anyway—"

There was a click and the door opened. Paul stood there blinking. "I shouted but no one came. I want a drink of water." When he saw Emily and Hubert he said without drawing breath, "Did you get my glasses?"

Hubert looked at Emily and Emily looked at her mother. "Did you find them, Mum? Under the hot plate on the sideboard."

Mrs. Hamilton looked at her daughter as if going bananas might have been catching. But Doctor Hamilton said with some impatience, "Come here, Paul, and sit down quietly. Go on, Hubert. We'll get the glasses sorted out afterward."

Hubert proceeded, and when he had come to the end, Doctor Hamilton said, "Why on earth didn't you bring her back with you? Even if she didn't want it, she obviously needs medical attention. All this rushing about with food and blankets—"

"We didn't rush about with blankets," said Emily. "They were there."

"I think your father means that if you had brought her straight here in the first place we could have had her in bed." She stopped and then added, "And we could have let her poor mother know."

Doctor Hamilton stood up. "I think I'd better go and get her. She might get a fright if ambulance men turned up. Hubert, you can show me the way. Emily, you'd better go to bed. And so had Paul when he's had his drink of water, which, of course, was just an excuse to get out of bed."

A howl rose from Paul, who dragged himself from his father and rushed into Mrs. Hamilton's arms. "I'm *thirsty*," he roared.

"Well, you shall have a nice cup of cocoa, and so shall Emily before she goes to bed," said Mrs. Hamilton in her most soothing tones.

But Hubert, who had been trying to speak, now said, "Emily!" in desperation, and Emily rushed to the door, and in the time-honored voice of high drama, shouted, "Wait!" They waited, more from surprise than obedience, and Emily said, "You better wait till Hubert explains. Go on, Hubert."

It was hard to convince Doctor Hamilton that even his benign presence might precipitate a crisis, even to the extent of Bianca's plunging into the dam once more. And besides, Hubert considered it would amount to a kind of betrayal, now that they had with such difficulty persuaded Bianca to trust them.

"Did she say her name was Bianca?" said Doctor Hamilton suddenly.

"Well, she had to have a name, Dad, and that was the first one she came up with. We don't know her real name. She doesn't remember," said Emily.

"But that's the curious thing," said Doctor Hamilton. "That *is* her name. Her mother told us."

After a long pause Hubert said, "We thought it was an odd name to choose, didn't we, Emily? But I'll swear she didn't really think it was her own."

"You see," said Doctor Hamilton, "it's not total amnesia."

"Total what?" said Emily.

"Dad means she hasn't forgotten everything, even if she thinks she has."

Emily nodded several times. "And there was the business about the cat, remember? Wasn't it beastly? Fancy remembering a thing like that."

"You'd better tell me," said Doctor Hamilton. So they told him and he became absorbed in thought for so long that Mrs. Hamilton eventually said, "I wonder, Hubert, if I were to go? Perhaps she needs mothering?"

Hubert said in a curiously remote voice, "That seems to be the last thing she wants." And as Emily nodded, continued, "She certainly didn't take to Emily, did she, Emily? Not noticeably, I mean." This time Emily rather sadly shook her head.

"Perhaps Emily's just not the motherly type," said Doctor Hamilton.

Mrs. Hamilton was about to rush to her daughter's defense, but Hubert said, "How would it be if we just left her to sleep quietly there tonight and Dad and I go out first thing in the morning? She might be OK after a night's sleep. She was improving bit by bit, wasn't she, Emily, by the time we left?"

"And she didn't expect anybody else tonight," said Emily. "Couldn't we leave her, Dad?"

But Doctor Hamilton's professional ethics would not allow him to wait until the morning, and in the end he got his bag, told Emily to go to bed at once or she would not be fit for school in the morning, and told Hubert to come with him. Paul was almost asleep again on his mother's lap, but opened his eyes at the general movement and said firmly, "My glasses, Emily."

Emily went out of the room in silence, returned, and in silence handed the glasses to Paul. She turned to her mother. "We had to think of some way to get back to that girl. It was my idea. It was the only way." She looked apprehensively at her father, but he only murmured, "Resourceful," and went out of the room.

As he and Hubert were leaving, Mrs. Hamilton said, "Oughtn't I to try to telephone the mother? I'd be surprised if she were asleep."

"I did think of that," said Doctor Hamilton, "but she

told me those thugs cut her telephone line, and I rather doubt that it's been fixed. You can try, but I think it'll have to wait till the morning. Perhaps better to wait till then anyway. We'll have more news of the girl."

"She'll have the whole night to get through," said Mrs. Hamilton, but all he said was, "Can't be helped."

"Bit tough on Emily," said Hubert as they emerged onto the road in the doctor's car. "She's damn good in a crisis, Emily. Always knows what to do."

"And tells you," said his father.

"But this was her thing, Dad, as well as mine. You wouldn't be going to the girl now if it wasn't for Emily. I wish she could have come."

He struggled with his sense of loyalty and continued to labor the point until Doctor Hamilton said, "For goodness sake, Hubert, what do you think this is? A game? The mother's nearly mad with worry, the girl's half out of her mind, and all you can think of is Emily's share in the, for want of a better word, excitement. Grow up."

A long silence followed this brutal speech while Hubert, who had honestly thought Emily would have contributed a good deal to the easing of the next hour or so, struggled hard to prevent himself saying so.

They were off the highway and onto the gravel side road when Doctor Hamilton began to speak again. Having said his say and thereby releasing a lot of pent-up anxiety, he was able to address his son in a more relaxed manner. "Come to think of it, Hubert, I don't suppose you would have heard about the woman who came to the office yesterday morning?" He told Hubert about Frances and the necessity of getting her daughter, somehow, away from the two thugs—out of danger—before they found out who she was. And of Frances's frantic search for Bianca afterward. "You can see, can't you, how a shock of this kind, acting on someone who was as sensitive as this girl must be, and who lived so isolated a life and so intimately with her mother and no one else, might easily have drastic results?"

Hubert, who was also sensitive, as Emily was not, could see very well and he felt a great pity for Bianca. "What will happen," he said, "when they meet again?"

"I'm wondering," said Doctor Hamilton.

Bianca heard them go. She heard the trailer door close, and she heard the car engine start, grow louder, and gradually diminish. She lay without moving until there was no sound at all. Then she sat up and pulled the blankets round her shoulders and tried to think. She had no idea how the cat story had suddenly floated into her mind. She had no idea where it had come from. But she knew it was something she had tried to forget. And now, when there were so many things she needed to remember, only that had come back. She tried to place it. Who, for instance, were "we"? She had said "we" when she spoke of it. And she remembered the shed where she had seen it. But who were "we"? The conviction suddenly came to her that the other person was female. She put her palms to her temples and pressed hard. She tried to will more pictures to come. For a long time she concentrated hard. But nothing came, and she fell back, mentally exhausted and sick with disappointment. Immediately another picture came to her. It was of a paddock, and somewhere in it, she knew, was a cow with its calf. She knew she was somehow involved with the cow and calf.

She sat up again and moaned and rubbed her face and looked about the trailer. But it was still quite dark and there was nothing to see. She could only smell its musty, airless smell. She thought hard about the paddock. She discovered she knew where the fence was, and she knew there was a creek somewhere at the bottom. Nothing else came, and she shivered with cold and slipped back under the blankets. This time she slept. After an hour she woke because the blankets had slipped off as she twisted in her sleep. With returning consciousness came a very vivid picture. It was of a door into a kitchen, and there were people in the kitchen. One face sprang into her mind. At first, confused and still disoriented, she could only think of the cat. But it was not the cat she was remembering now. And as she concentrated—on the cat, on the face that was not the cat's, on the kitchen she saw through the open door, the total blankness of no memory at all began to give way to more pictures. She found she knew there was another door on the other side of the kitchen. She knew where that door led. One of the rooms it led to was her own bedroom. It was not her own bed she was lying in now. But the face—she could still see the face. And it was her mother's.

A wave of pain went through her. She got out of bed and stood, shaking in the darkness. She put her hands over her face again and wished she had not remembered.

*   *   *

Hubert made his father leave the car some distance from the trailer. There was a flashlight in the glove compartment and they took it to light their way along the small winding track that led to the clearing. "I don't know how I'm going to explain bringing you," he said as they drew near. "All she can think of is getting away from everyone, even if it means getting drowned to do it. It was just luck and the fact that Emily hung on like grim death that made her accept us in the end."

"I hope you won't need to explain," said Doctor Hamilton. "You can go in first, and you must get her to swallow the capsules I've brought. Say you came back to give them to her, or something like that. They'll knock her out quite quickly and we can carry her to the car. She'll wake up in the hospital, sedated, and we can deal with her more gently."

It was not a plan that appealed to Hubert at all. The part he had to play was not pleasant. Now that he knew the whole story his inclination was to stand between Bianca and trouble, wherever it might come from, and however worthy the end result. He would not have called himself a knight errant, but his motives, romantic, unpractical, but heartfelt, were identical with theirs. Emily would have had no problem at all. "I don't like it," he said.

"Possibly not. But the decision is no longer yours."

They reached the edge of the clearing and stopped. Doctor Hamilton put four capsules into his hand. "Only two," he whispered. "Put the other two in your pocket in case anything goes wrong. Open the door and flash the light when you think it's right for me to come."

The trailer was still as they had left it—in total darkness. He opened the door quietly and went in. He did not switch the flashlight on immediately, but even without its light he knew at once that the trailer was empty. When he turned its beam to the bed he saw the tumbled blankets trailing from the bed across the floor where they had fallen as she made her escape. From what? No one could have come. There was no sign of disturbance. He went to the door and called his father. In the dead quiet of the night his voice cut like a blade, and somewhere overhead a bird squawked. His father was beside him in a moment and he said, "She's gone."

"Then we must look for her. At once. Has it occurred to you that there might be a quite simple explanation? That extraordinarily unsuitable food you and Emily brought her could well have had dramatic results. I just hope they weren't too violent."

"Oh, God. We never thought—at least, we did think, but there was nothing else."

"You could have brought her back."

"I told you—"

"Well, never mind. Now we must find her. Until it's light we'll do best by being quiet and listening."

They walked off in different directions making as little noise as they could and stopping every few minutes to listen. It was that dead hour of a moonless night when it was almost—but not quite—impossible to see anything.

But the day was not far off and soon the birds would begin again. Hubert hoped he would be the one to find her. He thought she would let him approach if he did so slowly enough. But his father had only one option—to grab her when he got the chance and hold on.

The shore of the dam was not far off, though where there were no tracks the scrub was thick. He found himself pushing toward it, for it seemed to him that he must reach it before he turned back to meet his father again in the clearing at the appointed time. There was still no sound, and he tried to use the light as little as possible, relying almost solely on his ears. When he stopped for the third time he sniffed the air and knew that the dam was not far off. Even if his father had to wait, he would make it now. And as he walked on he felt a lifting of the spirit. One by one the birds began to tell him the same thing, and, looking up and seeing the tops of the trees outlined against a transparency of darkness, he turned his flashlight off for the last time. He could see brief gleams of light through the bushes as he drew near the water. The dam would reflect the coming day at once and drive the last of this endless night away. He pushed more hurriedly and more carelessly through the scrub, until he saw that it ended only a short distance ahead, and the shore lay open and grassy to the bank. He was almost running, but suddenly he stopped short. In the half light a figure was standing on the brink of the water and he saw that it was Bianca. She was quite motionless and she was looking out across the dam. He wondered how much she had remembered in the night. He was about to call out, but stopped himself in time and instead began to step very cautiously to the edge of the bushes.

Emerging from it, he stood motionless, only the width of the grass verge away from her. She was very still, and her hands hung loose by her sides. Her head was raised, but he had a feeling that she saw nothing. She still did not know that he was there and he wondered what he should do next. In the end he said very softly, "Bianca, it's only me."

She gave a gasp, flung her head round, and saw him. Once again the panic was clear in her face. All the tranquillity of the night before had gone and the wild look was back in her eyes. Before he had time to move or speak, she leapt off the bank, shattering the still surface, and began to plunge out into deep water.

This time there was no Emily to send him involuntarily after her, but this time it was not necessary. He had been waiting, poised, to act as soon as he knew what she would do, and now he was after her and into the water almost before she had left the shallows. He pushed off with his feet, reached out, and caught her by the ankle as she began to swim. As he pulled her back her head went under, and she came up coughing. Now he got an arm round her waist, dragged her to the bank, and lifted her out. He climbed out himself, got to his knees, and looked into her face. To his amazement she smiled at him. She stopped coughing and said, "Thank you, Hubert."

He pulled her roughly to her feet. "What were you doing? What were you thinking of?"

"I—" She was not smiling anymore, and with an effort she said, "I remembered. In the night after you'd gone I remembered. I was trying to get away."

"But why into the dam? Why there? You'd never swim across."

"I didn't want to. I wasn't trying to swim across."

"What, then?" He waited, and wondered what her answer would be.

She pulled herself from him. "I don't know. I only thought it would be safe in the water. It seemed to be the only place left for me to go." She stopped, and he saw her eyes widen. "Was I mad? Hubert, was I mad?" She flung herself at him and he felt her clutching arms. "I'm not. I'm not mad." She buried her face in his wet shirt.

This was something Hubert was not prepared for. He stood now, acutely embarrassed, full of pity, totally at a loss. He stood and held her lightly, finding nothing to say, waiting until she recovered. When he felt her grow calmer he took her arms and unwound them, stepping back so that he could see her face. "You're not mad," he said. "But you gave a pretty good imitation of it. You could have fooled me."

She looked at him, stunned. Then she laughed. For one appalled moment he thought she was having hysterics. But she stopped as suddenly as she began. He took her hand and said, "It's going to be all right. Come with me to find my father. He'll be cross with me that he's had to wait so long."

She followed him obediently enough, but by the time

they reached the clearing she was far from laughter. His father was sitting on the step of the trailer. He got up as Hubert pushed his way through the scrub and began to say, "Hubert, I thought I told you—" and then saw Bianca follow him out of the bushes. She stopped and half turned when she heard his voice, and might have vanished again if Hubert had not taken her hand and held it tightly.

"It's only my father," he said. "He thought I'd be back sooner. I would have been if you hadn't gone jumping into the dam. You'd better come and tell him. Get me out of trouble."

She followed him then, and when they reached him, Doctor Hamilton said nothing more alarming than, "You're all wet."

Bianca shook herself free of Hubert and went and stood in front of him and said, "I fell into the dam. Hubert pulled me out. That's why we're wet." She spoke calmly, but Hubert could see her two hands clenched behind her back.

Doctor Hamilton made no comment, but opened the trailer door. "Come inside," he said. "It's warmer. We'll find some coffee. Sit down and wrap yourself in the blankets."

She did as she was told, and waited for the coffee. When it was ready Hubert took it and sat down beside her on the bed. Doctor Hamilton perched himself on the table. "Now," he said. "Can you tell me your name?"

She said at once, "Bianca Bellini."

"Your mother has been looking for you."

At once Hubert saw the look of panic in her eyes. "It's all right," he said quickly. "Nothing's going to happen," and wondered why he had said it. But he watched the panic fade.

When she spoke, her voice was controlled and positive. "I won't see her."

"Can you tell me why?" Doctor Hamilton drank his coffee while he waited for her answer.

"She hates me. That's why." She was looking at him warily, but she had taken hold of Hubert's hand and was holding it as if, again, he was saving her from drowning.

"Do you realize now, after thinking it over, that you made a mistake?"

"I don't know what you mean. I didn't have to think anything over. I saw her face." She began to shake, and Hubert, with the pretense of pulling the blanket up, put his arm round her shoulders.

"Wait," he said. "Wait till Dad tells you."

At that she twisted in his arm to face him and said savagely, "What do you know about it? You weren't there." Her sudden spurt of anger surprised them. Her self-control was still on a knife edge.

Doctor Hamilton said, "Neither was I there, but I was there when your mother was brought to my office. She told me herself what had happened."

Bianca was immediately suspicious. "I don't know why she should have been brought to your office. She's perfectly well."

"On the contrary. She was on the point of collapse."
"Why?"
"Because she had lost you."
For a moment Bianca looked at him incredulously.

Then, for the second time that morning, she laughed. But this time it was an ugly sound, full of scorn and, beneath the scorn, pain.

"It's true."

But now she did not believe him, and because Hubert was his son she began to draw away from him, too, and they could see by the way her eyes began to roam about the trailer that escape was in her mind again. Doctor Hamilton, watching Bianca's cup, spoke to Hubert. "What about another cup, Hubert? I thought we weren't going to need it, but I think, after all, it would be a good idea." And Hubert knew he was telling him the time for the capsules had come.

"Dad," he said, "would you let me talk to Bianca before—before we all have another cup? If you were perhaps just to wait at the door—?" To his surprise and relief, his father nodded.

"If you like," he said. "We've got all morning." And Hubert knew there would be confusion in the office and questions at the hospital. The weight of responsibility was suddenly heavy on his shoulders. He could have done with Emily and her unshakable sanity. Doctor Hamilton put down his mug and got up. He stretched and said, "I'll get a breath of air. I'll be just outside the door," and he looked closely at his son. There would be no chance of an escape, his look said.

When he had gone and the door was shut again, Hubert waited for a long time before he spoke. Bianca was now sitting bundled in her blankets with her arms wrapped across her stomach. Her head was bent and she seemed to have lost interest in everything, particularly Hubert. He wished he had not asked his father to leave. He had thought he could reassure Bianca, but now he was not so sure. She seemed to have withdrawn absolutely, and while his pity was no less, nor his wish to help, the insight into her mind that had helped him before had deserted him now. He did not know how to begin. At last he said, "If you don't want to go back to your mother, where will you go?"

Without looking up she said, "I don't know. And if I did know, I wouldn't tell you."

"Bianca." It was surprising how damaged he felt.

"I didn't know. I thought you were just—helping. You were trying to catch me, weren't you?"

"If you think stopping you getting drowned is trying to catch you—"

"I don't know what to think." She flung the blankets off and stood up. When she took a step toward the door Hubert was up and bringing her back to the bed before she had really decided what it was she intended to do. "You see?" she said. "You're keeping me prisoner—you and your father. All I've wanted has been to get away. I don't want to hurt anyone, or upset anyone. I just want to be left alone—because there's no one I can trust anymore."

"Oh, lord," said Hubert, and sighed. Then he took a deep breath and said, "Look, you're a silly, stupid girl and it's time you got hold of yourself. When your memory went you had some excuse for going on in this crazy way, but now you've remembered again you might as well start behaving like a human being and not something out of a cheap movie." He stopped, appalled at himself. But once again he had, unwittingly, found the one opening through her defenses. She was looking at him with her mouth open, and he saw the blood flood into her cheeks. Before she had time to say anything he sat down beside her and began talking. He deliberately made his voice flat and unemotional.

"I'm going to tell you how we live at home. Then if you want to, you can tell me how you live—used to live—" He stopped and waited for a reaction that did not come, and continued, "There's Emily and me and Dad, and you've met all of us. You know because we told you that Dad is a doctor. Then there's our little brother, Paul. You might have seen Paul that time you came out of the mist when we were all standing on the bank of the dam. And there's Mum. We live in a middle-sized house in a middle-sized town and Dad has a middle-sized practice." She had begun to listen, and he saw without turning his head that she was looking at him. "I'm nearly finished school and I'm going to study medicine when I leave. Emily's at school, too, and she's got a few more years to go. I don't know what she wants to do—something practical, like engineering, I expect. Paul's in primary and seems to be causing a certain amount of disturbance there. At present his aim in life is to become an unmanned space satellite. Being the youngest, he's spoiled, but on the whole, we like him." He saw the smallest of smiles cross her face. "Mum isn't a career woman, or anything like that, though she says she's going to be as soon as she gets the time. She'll never have time because we all need her. But if she does want to break out,

I'm going to see she can. I don't see why she should spend her life cooking for us. I expect we could all eat less, and I could cook things like scrambled eggs when I'm home. Emily's not bad on desserts, either. Mum could go off and be an airline stewardess, or something." He was rambling on because he had her attention now, but the idea of his ample mother as an airline stewardess suddenly appealed to him and he stopped to laugh.

"Go on," she said, and settled to listen again.

He told her all he could think of—the smallest items of their family life, down to the time the refrigerator exploded and the crisis with the laundry faucet. For the moment she seemed to have forgotten herself entirely in the minutiae of his family life. But he ran out of things to say in the end, and stopped and, taking a risk, said, "Now you tell me about your life."

He thought she was never going to start, but at last she began. She started with her memories of her father and explained about his love for the farm. She described their family life—the hard work, the animals, the excitement of being able to afford a washing machine. She told him of her father's death, and how she and her mother between them had decided to carry on with the farm, how she went to the local school and did her farm jobs when she came home in the afternoon. She started to tell him about the old gentleman who gave her music lessons. Then she stopped. He saw a completely new expression come over her face. She remained silent for so long that at last he said, "What is it? What's happened?" He knew that whatever it was, it was good, and there was no harm in asking.

"I forgot," she said. "How could I have forgotten? I've just passed my first music exam. I even got a distinction." It was the first time he had been able to glimpse the sort of person she might be when she was truly happy. It was a revelation. After a minute she continued, and brought her life right to the moment she walked toward the kitchen door. Then she stopped abruptly and a curtain came down over her face. "I can't tell you any more," she said, and ceased to look at him.

"Dad can tell you some things you don't know," said Hubert. "Shall I call him in? Would you like to hear them?" and held his breath for her answer.

It was not until he had decided she was not going to answer at all that she said, "Do you think I should?"

"You'd be happier if you did. Will you try?" And when at last she nodded he got up and went to the door and opened it. "Dad," he said as his father stepped into the trailer. "Bianca would like to hear everything that happened the other day at the farm. Will you tell her?"

So Doctor Hamilton sat himself down, made himself as comfortable as a trailer will allow, and began to tell her. He told it exactly as her mother had told him, and told her, too, how Frances had refused to stay in the hospital, but had run away and gone home when she was not yet well enough so that Bianca should not come back—if she came back—to an empty house. He stopped, and after a long silence, which she appeared to have no wish to break, he said, "Well, will you come back with us now? Your mother will be waiting."

She stood up, and he at once put himself between her

and the door. But it was not necessary. "I'll come back with you," she said. "But I don't think I want to see my mother." She looked at Hubert and said to him, "I'm frightened."

"You won't be," he said, "after a while. Come along, Bianca." And he took her arm and led her to his father's car. Over his shoulder he said, "I'll come back later and lock up the trailer when Mum doesn't need her car."

As he stepped into the car he heard his father's voice quietly in his ear. "Well done, Hubert."

By the time they reached the town the day's work had properly begun. It was a brisk and breezy morning and the streets were full of busy people, for a few brief hours at peace with all the world in the spring sunshine. Because there were so many people about, and in a town the size of theirs a doctor's activities are always of interest, he drove his car into the open garage. Bianca walked between them, supported on each side, up the garden path. They were halfway to the door when it opened and Mrs. Hamilton came running out.

"You're back at last. I was just beginning—" And now she saw the girl who walked between them. She stopped quite still, looked hard into her face, looked in turn at her husband and her son, took one more step forward, and opened her arms wide. "Come inside," she said. "Come and get warm." She spoke directly to Bianca, and Doctor Hamilton and Hubert simultaneously let her arms go.

For a moment Bianca swayed, and she looked at the large, smiling, welcoming figure before her, and suddenly ran, stumbling, and let herself be enfolded by Mrs. Hamilton's warm, plump arms. Over her head Mrs. Hamilton said, "I'll look after her now. You two go and get your breakfast. It's been ready for an hour. And Hubert, you'd better have a sleep. Your face has got that wrung-out dish-cloth look. Henry, there've been a lot of calls, but I said you'd ring back when you could. They're all on the pad."

She took Bianca inside, and Doctor Hamilton said, "We don't have to worry about *her* anymore. We'd better have our breakfast. Come on, Hubert."

11

They had almost finished breakfast, and Doctor Hamilton had already answered two more calls when Mrs. Hamilton came and sat down beside them at the breakfast alcove in the kitchen.

"Well?" said her husband.

"She's asleep. She'll sleep for a long time. There were tears—a good thing—and then she just dropped off, as if she'd been hit on the head. I've put her into a pair of Emily's pajamas and I'll wash her wet things. She feels safe now, so she'll be all right. Poor little creature. She must have been nearly out of her mind."

"She was," said Doctor Hamilton dryly. Then he added, "If it hadn't been for Hubert—he somehow got onto her wavelength—we'd have had a lot more trouble."

"Oh, Hubert!" said Mrs. Hamilton warmly.

"I know it sounds odd," said Hubert. "It's usually Emily."

"I didn't mean that at all. You know I didn't, Hubert."

"Yes, you did, Ma." He touched her lightly on the shoulder. "But I don't mind. Could I have another egg? It's been a long night."

Doctor Hamilton got up. "I'll have to go. Keep the child sleeping as long as you can. By the way, did you manage to get on to Mrs. Bellini?"

Mrs. Hamilton looked worried. "I tried and tried, but her phone's still out. I left a message at the exchange. It was the best I could do."

He nodded, thinking. At the door he said, "I'll get someone at the police station to bring her in, I think. The sooner we get them together the better."

He was already out of sight when Hubert said, "Dad. Wait." When Doctor Hamilton's head reappeared, Hubert said, "Could you leave it for a bit—till we sort things out? I think we should talk to the girl—to Bianca first."

"Do you? Why?"

"You remember she said she was frightened? She is. She's still frightened of facing her mother."

"Oh, poor child," said Mrs. Hamilton.

"Well, leave it till I come back at lunchtime. I think we'd better talk it over. 'Bye," and he was really gone.

"If he comes back at lunchtime," said Hubert.

His mother looked at him. "Hubert, you've got awfully wise all of a sudden."

He smiled. "Surprising, isn't it? Matter of fact, I do feel sorry for the kid. She seems so helpless—lonely—you know. Fancy trying to drown herself."

"Hubert! She didn't!"

"She says not. Some lunatic notion of being safe in the water. Mum, she *is* a bit odd."

"So would you be, Hubert, if you'd led the sort of life she's led and then had that happen to you. I'm sorry for her, but I'm more sorry for her mother. So what do you think we should do about her mother, Hubert? She must be told, you know, and she's sure to want to see the child."

"Could you go and talk to her? In your car—now?"

"Yes. That'd be the—" Then she shook her head. "I can't. I really don't dare leave this child. She might wake up."

"Should I go?"

"It's an idea. No. We said we'd wait till lunchtime. We'll do that. And in the meantime—" She suddenly became brisk. "For goodness sake go and have a shower and get some sleep. You look dirty and half dead."

"I'm both," said Hubert. "Good night, Ma."

By lunchtime a slight complication had arisen. Paul, who had been thought sufficiently recovered to go back to school, and who should have been safely disposed of until three o'clock at least, turned up with a high color and a note from his teacher. She said she feared he might have something catching, and would his father please check.

Mrs. Hamilton looked at him over the top of her glasses. "What have you been doing, Paul?"

"Nothing, Mum. Honest. Nothing. I only told Miss Perkins my head felt buzzy. She asked if I felt funny. I had to tell the truth, didn't I?"

"Of course." She looked at him closely. "Was it buzzy?"

"Well, it was a bit." A small discomfort made him wriggle. "See, Noel punched me—on the head."

"Whatever for?" It was the kind of conversation Mrs. Hamilton was always having with her younger son.

"I only sort of went to sleep and my head kind of fell on his exercise book."

At this point Mrs. Hamilton put her hand on his forehead. "Oh dear," she said. "I hope it isn't anything catching. You'd better go to bed till your dad comes home."

"I don't want to." Paul's face became redder than ever and his voice was very loud.

"Shsh!" she said, and put her hand over his mouth. "Be quiet, Paul. There's someone sleeping—oh heavens, she's sleeping in your bed." She sighed. "Oh well, come along. You'll have to go into my bed."

As this had always been regarded as a special privilege, Paul stopped protesting at once and meekly followed his mother to the bedroom. As she put him into bed, he said, "Who's in my bed, Mum?"

"That girl. The one you saw on the dam. They've found her again."

He was interested at once. "Can I see her? Just once? Before I go to bed? Do let me."

"And sprinkle her with all the germs you might have? Of course not. You shall see her later. And Hubert's asleep, too. He's been up all night. So you must be quiet," she said quickly, as he showed signs of getting out of bed again. "What do you want to eat? Ice cream?"

"Gee, yes, thanks, Mum." He slid down between her sheets and heaved a sigh. "It's not too bad here, Mum. My head does buzz a bit." And as she watched, his eyes closed. She walked back to the kitchen through a houseful of sleeping people and wondered what on earth she could get them all for lunch. She also wondered what nasty disease Paul could be about to precipitate on his family.

Doctor Hamilton did turn up for lunch. He turned up late, but he turned up. He was glad he had, for there was quite a large lunch. Mrs. Hamilton had provided for five, but when lunchtime came three of the five were still deeply asleep, and it seemed to be madness not to snatch the rare opportunity of a peaceful meal and a quiet talk together.

"So did you work out anything with Hubert about Mrs. Bellini? We really can't leave it any longer."

"What do you think about Hubert's taking my car and going to see her this afternoon? It sounds cruel, but from what you and Hubert have told me, I'm inclined to think we should keep the child here for a while, and take her home when she's ready to go. Could it wreck everything to bring her mother here to confront her while she's in this state? Go on, you're the doctor." Sometimes Mrs. Hamilton liked to indulge in a mild form of bullying when she especially wanted her husband to take decisive action.

He was hungry, late for his meal, and busy with his knife and fork. She had to wait for his answer. It came eventually in the form of a question. "If you were the girl's mother, would you wait? Could you wait?"

She thought for a long time. At last she said, "If it were properly explained to me why I had to wait, yes, I would. I wouldn't like it. I should hate it. And it would be difficult. But I would wait."

Doctor Hamilton nodded, and, when he had finished his meal, wiped his mouth, and sat back in his chair, he said, "You know, I think that would be best. I think Hubert should go and see her. Actually, Hubert's come out of this rather well. He mightn't be as practical as Emily, but he's shown a lot of perception over this girl."

"I always told you there was more to Hubert, apart from his brains, than you gave him credit for." She was very smug.

"Yes. Well." His effort not to smile was unsuccessful. But he was quite serious again when he said, "So let Hubert go as soon as he wakes up, but he must understand that if he can't manage to persuade her—and it's certainly going to be difficult—he's to bring her in if she insists. And we'll face the consequences when they arise."

Before he left again he looked at Paul. As it turned out it was not necessary to wake him up. Doctor Hamilton, having felt his forehead, gently opened his pajama front and revealed a flourishing crop of little pink spots. "Chicken pox," he said. "There's a lot of it about."

"Oh, good grief," said Mrs. Hamilton. "Now what do we do?"

"Just keep him in bed. I'll do all that's necessary. Better notify the school. All in the day's work."

"But what about the girl? The infection?"

"If she's had it she won't get it. If she hasn't, she might as well have it now as some time when she's pregnant later on."

"It only needed this," said Mrs. Hamilton, and for the first time showed signs of wilting.

Doctor Hamilton's parting words were, she thought, unkind. "If Hubert doesn't wake pretty soon, you'll have to wake him. We can't leave this too long." And he went off to his office.

Mrs. Hamilton did not exactly wake Hubert, but she contrived to make quite a lot of noise just outside his bedroom door, and in the end—and quite soon enough, she thought—he tottered out looking dazed and as if he were not yet in control of his leg muscles. She brought him a cup of strong coffee and told him he must dress at once. As soon as he had managed to grasp what she was telling him he did so quickly, and when he was ready he said, "Now. How do I get there?"

She gave him the notes that Doctor Hamilton had jotted down before he left, told him exactly what his father had said, and went out with him to the car. "Be careful," she said. "Be kind. And be firm—but not too firm. Oh, and by the way, Paul has the chicken pox."

"Paul always manages to get in on the act somehow. 'Bye, Ma." And he went.

12

The drive to Frances Bellini's house took him nearly two hours, and in that time he did a good deal of thinking. And the more he thought, the more he felt his confidence ebbing away. He had no trouble, following the diagram his father had left, in finding his way, but as he turned off the paved road onto the gravel one, he found himself wishing the distance had been twice as far. He did not even know what Frances looked like. He knew he would find her overwrought and he would be embarrassed. He could never cope with emotional displays. It was only by remembering Bianca and her great and immediate difficulties that he could keep his foot firmly on the accelerator.

He came to the farm at about three-thirty in the afternoon. The day had continued as it had promised—fine, calm, and with the first breaths of summer on the quiet air. He had not given much thought to what Frances's reaction might be when she saw his car draw up by the farm gate, but he thought of it now, and knew that a number of wild hopes as well as fears would go near to overwhelming her as soon as she saw it. It was better to be quick. He turned off the engine, slammed the car door, and walked fast through the gate and up the path to the back door. It opened before he reached it.

"It's all right," he said almost before he reached her. "She's safe. But she's not with me." And he saw the sudden light die out of her eyes. "May I come in?"

She walked ahead of him, looking dazed, and the first thing she did was to put the kettle on. And he knew that if he had told her they had found Bianca's body she would have done the same thing. He stood, uncertain, in the doorway. "May I come in? I have to talk to you."

She whirled round. "What? What's happened?"

He realized he must not let himself be hurried. "I'm Hubert, Doctor Hamilton's son. We—my sister and I— found Bianca down by the dam. She's quite all right. We brought her home. She's in bed." He saw her eyes widen and continued hurriedly. "She's just tired. Mum's looking after her." He thought she relaxed at that, but he had not finished speaking before she interrupted.

"Why didn't you bring her? Why hasn't she come home?"

So now the difficult part came. How to tell her that her daughter did not want to come home? He did the best he could. "Mum said to tell you she thinks it would be better if Bianca was properly rested before coming home. And Dad"—he decided the fabrication was justified—"Dad said he'd like to keep an eye on her for a bit. See, Mrs. Bellini, she was terribly tired and terribly hungry when we found her." He did not think it necessary to tell her Bianca had twice plunged herself into the dam, nor that she had temporarily lost her memory. Time enough for his father to tell her that, and to explain its cause. He thought he was doing fairly well, for she was listening with her eyes fixed on his face, not attempting to interrupt, but suddenly she sprang to her feet.

"Well, I'll get my coat and bag and you can take me to your house, can't you? I'm ready to go now."

There was no way he could avoid telling her. "I'd rather not do that, Mrs. Bellini."

She stood in the open doorway that led into the passage with her back to him. "Why not? Why can't you?"

He had to be brutal. "Bianca doesn't want to see you—yet. She's frightened. She told me she was frightened."

She turned very slowly and he thought he had never seen a face with quite that expression before—except, perhaps, on Bianca's face. He hoped he was going to be able to forget it. He had a feeling it was going to remain with him. But his job was to remove it now, if he could.

"You see, she's sort of shocked. She doesn't know what to think. Dad believes it will be safer to wait until she's ready to come home—until she asks to come home. You do see, don't you, Mrs. Bellini?"

"For goodness sake call me Frances." The anguish in her voice had nothing to do with whatever he might choose to call her.

He could not make matters worse now, so he went on doggedly, "Dad said I was to bring you back if you insisted, but he did ask me to try to persuade you not to come."

She came and sat down at the table. For a long time she looked at the hands twisting in her lap, while Hubert waited. Then at last, like Bianca before her, she said, "What shall I do?" and she looked up at him.

"Just wait. And make the house nice and ready for her."

"I don't know. I *want* to see her. She's my daughter."

"Are you coming, then?"

He thought she was not going to answer at all, but after a long time she said, "No." If he had not been listening carefully he would not have heard her answer.

Hubert got up. "We'll be in touch with you every day as soon as your phone's fixed. To tell you how she is. I'm sure it won't be long. We'll look after her, Mrs.—Frances." She said nothing, and sat there looking at her hands again, but now they were not twisting together. This time, Hubert noticed, they lay like dead birds in her lap. At the door he stopped. "Ought to tell you. Paul—my little brother—he's got chicken pox. Dad said it wouldn't matter about Bianca. If she's had it she won't get it, and if she hasn't and does get it, it will be a good thing on account of not getting it later when she's pregnant and all that."

For a moment she looked at him wildly. Then she relaxed. "Oh, thank you," she said. "That *is* kind."

Hubert thought of something else—something to leave with her when he left. "Bianca told me about the music exam. Mrs.—Frances, she was really excited and happy."

Perhaps it had been the wrong thing after all, for she suddenly turned her face away from him, got up, and went out of the kitchen.

Hubert had had enough. He had had all he could take

for the moment and all he wanted was to get home again. As he drove out of the yard and onto the track he saw the cow making her way up to the paddock gate, with her calf trying to butt at her udder as she walked. It relieved him to know he would not find Frances still sitting at the kitchen table if he returned. The cow would soon begin to remind her that she had duties to perform.

He got home to find Emily giving instructions to his mother on the best way to nurse chicken pox. Mrs. Hamilton was smiling and saying, "Yes, Emily. Yes, dear," as she set the dinner table. His interview had left his nerves jangled and he said with rather more asperity than he need have, "You may remember, Emily, that you have had chicken pox, I have had chicken pox, and I dare say Mum has had chicken pox. What makes you think she needs your advice?"

"Oh, Hubert," said Emily, allowing his words to brush off her. "How did you get on? What was it like? What's she like?" Mrs. Hamilton stopped setting the table and walked over to the door.

When she had shut it she said, "Tell us now, Hubert. Was it awful for you? I see you haven't got her with you."

"I suppose it was no more awful than I expected," said Hubert. "But I don't want to have to do it again. Someone else can go next time. I think you'd better go."

Mrs. Hamilton nodded. "I will. But I hope there won't be a next time. You did well, Hubert, if you persuaded her to wait."

"It was a bit like flaying her alive," said Hubert as casually as he was able.

"No need to exaggerate," said Emily.

To her surprise Mrs. Hamilton turned on her. "You don't know what you're talking about, Emily. Hubert sees, better than you do, what all this means to that woman." It was seldom Mrs. Hamilton allowed herself to show signs of real anger.

Hubert said quickly. "How's Paul, anyway? How's that scrofulous boy?"

She recovered at once. "Enjoying all the amenities of the sickbed. Go and see him if you like, Hubert. He'll like that. He'll only see you as a blob of pink cotton wool, I expect. He's got a spot coming on his nose and finds his glasses uncomfortable. He doesn't really need cheering up, because he feels too important, but he'd like to see you."

For the next few days life in the Hamiltons' house settled into a busy, but a less eventful, routine. Paul's disease pursued its normal course and, not without difficulty, he was discouraged from scratching his spots. Every morning Mrs. Hamilton telephoned Frances to report on Bianca's well-being. Frances never asked the one question that never left her mind. But Mrs. Hamilton never put down the receiver without saying, "Not long now, Frances," and hoped it was true. Bianca began slowly to recover her physical health and her mental stability. And each day she showed signs of increased happiness. But each evening Doctor Hamilton asked his wife if she had given any sign that she would like to see her mother and each evening Mrs. Hamilton had to say, "Not yet."

One day during office hours Doctor Hamilton's secretary, "rolling her eyes," as he told his wife afterward, came in to say that Mrs. Bellini was in the waiting room. He was glad to see her when she came in and told her so. "You should have stayed in the hospital until I had seen you, you know."

She looked thinner than he remembered, and her deep-set eyes told of wakeful nights. And she found it hard to sit still. But she spoke calmly enough. "I know. And I have to apologize. But I couldn't just lie there. I couldn't."

"I'm glad you felt well enough to leave. How are you now?"

"Well enough. I've only just got my vehicle back, or I would have come before. I—" Suddenly she stopped.

If she was going to ask to see Bianca he would have to dissuade her somehow. But she did not. All she said eventually was, "I've brought some clothes for Bianca. Is that all right? May I leave them here?"

He had not thought it wise to tell her very much until now, but here was the obvious opportunity, and he began to explain how Bianca had been found. She had to know about the loss of memory and he told her as gently as he could. But she sat bolt upright, fixed him with those bruised eyes, and kept her hand over her mouth. She only relaxed when he finished by saying, "It's perfectly all right now. She remembers everything, though she doesn't like talking about it much, and it only lasted for a very short time."

"I had to do it." It was a plea for reassurance.

He gave it to her at once. "Of course you had to do it. And in the same circumstances you would do it again, wouldn't you?"

She nodded. But after a moment she said, "But I didn't know—if I'd known—"

"You would still have done it, and it would still have been the best course. But now you must be patient. I am sure she will feel differently in time. But you must give her time."

The days went by, and each day, they thought, showed a small improvement. Bianca got on wonderfully well with Paul. She read to him, she told him stories, and, to everyone's surprise, she sang to him—little haunting Italian tunes that she must have learned from her father. It was Hubert who noticed that sometimes she would stop in the middle of one of them. There would be a long silence until Paul broke it.

"Go on, Bianca. Sing some more."

No one ever heard her sing a German song.

Paul's glasses remained on the table by his bed. With Bianca to entertain him he did not need them. "You look like a sort of fuzzy flower when you come in at the door," he said. "I like it."

It was the nights that now began to reveal a deep disturbance that at first only Hubert guessed at. Bianca's nightmares began again. Mrs. Hamilton, passing her room one night on the way to bed, heard what she thought was the sound of stifled crying. When she opened the door the sound revealed itself as a kind of soft wailing, and in the wailing were distinguishable words. She went noiselessly to the bed. Bianca was lying quite still and in the faint light from the passage Mrs. Hamilton could see that her eyes were closed. The sounds, coming from half-closed lips, were muffled. Only one thing was clear: the deep desolation they held within them.

The clear evidence of pain was more than Mrs. Hamilton could bear and, very gently, she put her hand on Bianca's shoulder. The sounds stopped immediately, but Bianca's eyes remained closed. She gave Bianca's shoulder a little shake, and saw the eyes slowly open. Bianca looked up, saw the face bending over her, and screamed.

"No, Mummy. No!"

Her scream woke the whole house, and in a moment Doctor Hamilton was at the door. He switched on the light and saw his wife trying to hold Bianca, while the girl writhed in terror. He went quickly to the bed.

"Let me," he said, and as his wife stepped back he lifted Bianca until she was sitting up, and gradually her struggles stopped. When she was quite still he said, "It's all right, Bianca. You were only dreaming."

But it took her a long time to settle again. Every so often she took a long, shuddering breath and her eyes began to roam about the room. In the end it was Hubert who sat beside her and held her hand until she slept again. After that first time it was always Hubert who would go to wake her and to sit beside her until she slept. He told his father the story of the cat and its kittens that he and Emily had heard in the trailer, and Doctor Hamilton said Frances must be told that Bianca could not return until the nightmares had stopped.

"I'm not going to tell her," said Hubert.

"Of course not. I'll ask your mother to do that. Not an easy thing."

"How are you going to stop the nightmares?"

"I really don't know yet. It's probably a matter for a psychiatrist."

In the end it was Hubert who stopped the nightmares and made it possible for Bianca to go home. He began by choosing the most prosaic situation possible—when they happened to be sitting in the car in the supermarket parking lot waiting for Mrs. Hamilton to finish her shopping. A cat walked across the parking lot and settled itself on the warm hood of the car beside them.

"Look, Hubert. She's done that before." Bianca's voice was quite relaxed and she watched the cat with mild amusement.

"An old hand," said Hubert. He looked carefully at Bianca for a moment and then said, taking a long breath, "You know, Bianca, all animals make mistakes sometimes. The cat you saw eating its kittens was doing what quite a lot of animals do by mistake. Instinct tells them to eat the afterbirth. People think it's so that other animals won't find out where the kittens, or whatever it may be, are and hurt them. Sometimes they go too far, especially if they're frightened. That's all." He stopped. Bianca had become very still. He waited, holding his breath.

When at last she looked at him and said, "Is that true?" in a tone that held nothing worse than surprise, he laughed aloud with relief.

"Of course it's true. Why else would I tell you?" And when Mrs. Hamilton returned to the car they were discussing television shows.

After that the nightmares became less frequent. "Now try to get her talking," Doctor Hamilton said to Hubert. "No one else seems to be able to." But when Mrs. Hamilton told Frances of the signs of improvement and Frances at last asked her question, she still had to say, "Not yet."

It was not easy to get Bianca alone. Emily felt it her personal duty to see at all times to Bianca's wants. But Emily, who might be thought to have a good deal more in common with Bianca than Hubert, being similar both in age and sex, could never break through the impenetrable curtain that Bianca put up between herself and the world. Emily had a regrettable habit of bouncing into Bianca's bedroom loudly exclaiming, "And how are we all today?" that was no help at all, and of feeling faintly hurt when Bianca failed to respond.

"A bedside manner," Hubert told her, "is not only unnecessary, but offensive." And Emily would flounce out until, quickly forgetting, she would do the same thing again.

Mrs. Hamilton stepped in and, choosing times when Emily was otherwise engaged, organized outings in the car for Hubert and Bianca. At first they went short distances at night and their conversation was spasmodic and trivial, and Hubert did not dare to broach any significant topic. When he suggested that Bianca might like to see more than the nighttime aspect of open paddocks and country roads she agreed to start a little before sunset instead of a little after. In this way he gradually accustomed her to longer and more interesting excursions. She was always drawn to the dam.

"Why?" said Hubert.

"It's where I feel safe," was always her puzzling reply.

He never pressed her to talk, but of her own accord she began to tell him things about the early days on the farm. When she mentioned his name, Hubert asked her about her father. She told him everything she could remember, and he could see that it pleased her to talk about Tony. One day she mentioned her mother. She seemed to forget her fear as she told Hubert about her mother's singing career and of the songs Tony loved her to sing.

"There was a special German one Daddy loved."

"Can you sing it to me?"

She began—"Herz, mein Herz"—and stopped dead, and tears suddenly ran down her cheeks. They had reached the bank of the dam, and Hubert stopped the car and while they were sitting there looking out over the placid sheet of water she told him of Tony's end and of how she had sat hour after hour singing that song until he died. "I should have gone for help," she said. "But I couldn't. He held me so tight."

Hubert had been sitting silent, more moved than he had thought possible. But at that he said almost angrily, "You should not have gone for help. Can't you see that was what he wanted? You made him happy. What more could he want at a time like that?"

"Are you sure? Oh, Hubert, thank you." She spoke as

if a great, aching pain had suddenly been lifted. Hubert felt the weight of an enormous and undeserved gratitude.

But after that he began to ask her questions. He asked none about recent happenings, but kept her occupied telling him of her own activities on the farm. Remembering the successful music examination, he asked her about the man who taught her music.

"Mr. Greville? He is so kind and so clever. Imagine all he's done for me." She stopped and then said, "I wish I could see him again. I had forgotten all about him. Could I?"

"Considering what else you forgot, it's hardly surprising." And they both laughed, and Hubert felt that at last perhaps he was getting somewhere.

That night when he was sitting alone with his father, he asked if anything was known of Mr. Greville.

"He's come several times to the office to ask after Bianca. He keeps telling me to handle her carefully. I don't know what he thinks we're doing—bashing common sense into her, or something. But he also talks of her precarious emotional balance, whatever that may mean." Hubert did not interrupt, but he knew what the music teacher meant. He had seen for himself that balance overthrown. Doctor Hamilton went on, "I suggested he should call on Frances because, heaven knows, this is the time Frances needs friends. But some sort of delicacy prevents him. He says he'd very much like her to come and see him, but nothing, it seems, will persuade him to go out to the farm for fear he'd be intruding."

"Do you know where he lives?"

"I can find out. Why?"

"I believe I'd like to go and see him."

"Why not? Yes, do go, Hubert. Something might come of it."

So Hubert went alone on the next weekend to visit Mr. Greville. They talked for a long time and when Hubert left, it was with a feeling that immense decisions had been reached—good or bad, it was impossible to guess.

A week went by, and it was only occasionally now that the nightmares came. The following Sunday Hubert took Bianca driving again. This time they went farther than usual and, as they proceeded, Bianca straightened her back and began to look about her. An increasing anxiety at last made her turn to Hubert.

"Hubert, where are we going? Are you taking me— you—"

"No," he said at once. "Not what you think. I have a surprise, and you are going to like it. Just wait."

When he turned down the road to Mr. Greville's house the frown suddenly left her face. "Now I know," she said, and sank back. "You are clever, Hubert. You knew."

"I guessed. And I hope—" He stopped and looked fixedly at the road ahead.

"What, Hubert?"

"Nothing." He looked at her quickly and, smiling, said, "We'll wait and see, shall we?"

But he was frowning when he watched her run through the small garden and up to the front door. Now that it was upon him, he very much wanted to turn back.

Mr. Greville opened the door before she had time to

knock. She flung her arms around him and Hubert saw the gray head bent over the flaxen one while the hands gently patted her back. As they went inside, Mr. Greville and Hubert exchanged a look before Mr. Greville said, "Into the sitting room today, Bianca."

When they were comfortably settled, Mrs. Greville brought in the tea and Hubert was introduced. Mrs. Greville was small and slight, and she, too, had gray hair. But there was a shrewd, smiling look in her eye that revealed a good deal of quiet wit and understanding. Bianca seemed as relaxed with her as she was with Mr. Greville. Cups of tea were passed, sandwiches handed round by Hubert. Inevitably they talked at first about the weather. Conversation proceeded along impersonal lines. Then Bianca said, "May I go into the music room? I haven't touched a piano since—since"—she took a breath—"for a long time now."

Mr. Greville said quite firmly, "After tea. After tea you can go into the music room. Someone is using it now—to practice." His voice was smooth and calm.

"Now, dear," said Mrs. Greville briskly, "a piece of cake?"

Hubert found himself without words. The conversation flowed over his head and he felt his nerves growing tight. At last Mrs. Greville got up, collected the empty cups, and was about to pick up the tray when Hubert said, "Let me."

"No, Hubert," said Mr. Greville at once. "You stay here, please."

Mrs. Greville lifted the tray and looked over the top of it at her husband. "Dear—shall I—?"

"When you have taken the tray out, you might just see if the music room is free, would you?"

She left the room and there was a short pause before Mr. Greville said, "Now, Bianca, when are you planning to start your music lessons again?"

She had seemed happy and untroubled here in the Greville's sitting room, but now a vitality, a radiance that Hubert had not seen before came over her face. "It's the one thing I want, Mr. Greville. May I—will you—when can I start?"

"Now, if you like," he said. "But you must just wait until my—visitor—has finished practicing."

As if on a cue, the sound of singing came, and Hubert guessed Mrs. Greville had opened the door of the music room. At first it was so soft they hardly heard it, but it grew in volume and now a melody became discernible. Mr. Greville stopped talking. He and Hubert sat very still. They had been looking at each other, but now both moved their heads very slightly to watch Bianca.

At first she sat listening calmly, waiting for the sound to develop, happy to be hearing music. As it grew louder her eyes widened, she lifted her head, and they could tell that gradually the whole of her awareness, her consciousness, was in her hearing. She saw nothing, and it was clear that her surroundings were forgotten.

The melody developed as the voice grew stronger, and now they could hear the words: "*Herz, mein Herz, warum so traurig?*—Oh my heart, why are you so sad?" The song continued and as verse followed verse the feeling in the words became stronger. Sentimental sadness changed to desolation. The mournful phrases took on the throb of passionate tragedy. The sound poured out now from the music room, strong and pleading. If it had ever been simply a sentimental drawing room song it was so no longer.

Bianca left her chair and moved like an automaton to the door. They saw her stand for a moment before opening it. Now the sound of singing was louder. She followed it, crossed the passage and went through the open door of the music room. There was a crash as the player's hands fell onto the keys and the singing stopped in midphrase. There came a long silence.

After that it seemed to Hubert that they sat just as they were for a very long time. Then, hearing a small sound, they both looked up. Frances and Bianca stood together in the doorway and Frances's arm was round Bianca's shoulders. Both were smiling, but the cheeks of both were wet. No words occurred to anyone, but there was no need. The kitchen door opened again and Mrs. Greville came in once again with a tray. She put it down with a small clatter and said, "Come along now, both of you. Sit down. Hubert, come and help me with the tea. It's a new brew. I thought we might all be glad of it."

Joan Phipson was born in Sydney, Australia, but spent much of her early life traveling in Europe and India with her parents. She first attended school in India, then in England and finally in Australia, where she was a pupil at Frensham School and later a librarian there. After studying journalism by correspondence, she worked for Reuters in London. Returning to Australia, she served in the Woman's Auxiliary Australian Air Force as a telegraphist before she married Colin Fitzhardinge and settled on their property in Central Western New South Wales. Many of her books reflect that countryside.

Joan Phipson's reputation as an author of books for children and young people has been widely recognized both in Australia and internationally. Her books have twice won the Children's Book Council of Australia Children's Book of the Year award and other of her titles have been Commended and Highly Commended in these same awards. Her *Watcher in the Garden* received an IBBY

Honor Diploma. *Hit and Run* was chosen as a White Ravens Selection of the International Youth Library in Munich. In the United States, it was chosen for the ALA Notable Books list for children and for the ALA Best Books list for young adults.